A LONG NIGHT'S JOURNEY INTO DAY

GROWING UP IN NAZI GERMANY

HERBERT A. GOERTZ

PAGE PUBLISHING
Conneaut Lake, PA

First originally published by Page Publishing 2022

ISBN 978-1-6624-8514-5 (pbk)
ISBN 978-1-6624-8515-2 (digital)

Printed in the United States of America

Our soul is escaped
as a bird out of the snare of the fowlers:
the snare is broken,
and we are escaped.

—Psalm 124:7

FOREWORD

Sadly, we live at a time when prejudices are again in ascendance. White supremacists are unashamedly blaring their hateful messages. Former Present Donald Trump has referred to African nations as *shithole* countries. He has branded Mexicans as rapists and killers, dismissed asylum seekers as invading hordes, and called immigrants an infestation. Moreover, a few years ago, apparently unable to accept the possibility that the United States might be led by a Black man, he came up with the trumped-up, baseless charge that Barack Obama had been born abroad and thus was ineligible for the office of president. Let these examples be a wake-up call to all who have deluded themselves into believing that such blatant prejudice is a thing of the past. Quite the contrary, it is alive and well. It is therefore important to remind ourselves constantly of the evils of Nazism whose racial ideology proclaimed the superiority of the Aryan race over all others. We know the horrors this kind of thinking brought into the world.

In view of these developments, my recollections of growing up in Nazi Germany have become unexpectedly timely again. My hope is that this book will serve as a warning against all forms of racism. It is an account of my journey through childhood into adolescence. It covers a scant ten years, but within this span of time lies a world of experience, poles apart. In the beginning, I am an innocent young boy on an island vacation. By the end, I have eaten of the tree of knowledge of good and evil and learned to what depths man can fall. The earth was drenched in blood. Weeds grew in the ruins of our habitations, and darkness was upon the face of the land.

Growing up in Nazi Germany was an unhinging experience which turned all my values and beliefs upside down, wrong side up. Of course, I sometimes lost my way in the blackness of the night and sometimes, was led astray by the false light of burning books and torchlight parades under the swastika banner. But I never lost my soul outright to the powers of darkness, for my parents were there to guide me. When the earth trembled, their love gave me a firm foundation on which to stand. When my head spun in hopeless confusion, their character, wisdom, and example set my thinking straight. When midnight threatened to engulf me, they pointed to the dawn of a new day. And so I dedicate this book to the memory of my father and my mother who kept me from being shattered on the deadly cliffs of Nazism. They lit a beacon to chart my course in the most difficult period of my life and saw to it that my journey did have a safe destination.

My parents were not heroes. They did nothing to openly oppose the Third Reich, but I will always be thankful to them because, in a raging sea of evil, they created a private island of stability where honor and decency could survive. That's not much perhaps in the eyes of the historian. To me, it made all the difference.

I have deliberately refrained from doing any research before writing this book. I wanted to tell the events as I remember them. They have stayed strong and fresh in my mind as if they happened only yesterday. No doubt my memory has played some tricks on me, mixing early and later levels of awareness in a kaleidoscope of time distortion, lengthening or foreshortening some recollections through the perspective of hindsight. This is no way diminishes the truth of these pages, which are a faithful account of my experience of growing up in Nazi Germany and what it did to me.

CHAPTER 1

I was rather proud of myself as we hurried to the beach promenade. There was going to be a fireworks display that my parents had sought to conceal from Hermann and me. Only Marita, twenty-two months older than I, had been asked to accompany them. Her great age conferred on her occasional privileges which I jealously strove to usurp for myself. Wasn't a seven-year old boy man enough to stay up late at night and still be his usual wide-awake self next morning? I certainly thought so, and when I heard some suspicious noises next door, I rushed over to investigate. Finding my sister and parents ready to leave for some unknown adventure, I insisted on going along. If they refused, I would cry and rouse my younger brother. That threat brought my parents' quick assent to my demand. Quietly I slipped into my clothes, and presently, we were strolling among a gay crowd of vacationers on the East Frisian Island of Borkum.

My guilt for having betrayed Hermann was soon forgotten in the excitement of the fireworks: crackling explosions, magical shapes thrust into the sky and falling down in a shower of sparks, a whirlwind of fiery stars, and worlds in collision. Never before had I seen such a marvelous display.

I did not know then that explosions and bursts of fire would soon lose their fascination for me and that tongues of flames licking across a blazing sky would come to mean terror and death to a small, frightened boy.

We were vacationing on Borkum. My father's serious air seemed oddly out of tune with the general holiday mood and his own customary good humor. For hours on end, he brooded over the daily papers with a worried look. On September 1, 1939, I knew what had been on his mind—war.

Three days later, we were on a boat to the port of Emden. Thousands of summer guests were fleeing the island headlong. The ship was crowded, yet it was strangely subdued and quiet on board. People stared anxiously into the sea, whispering about British mines and submarines.

When we got back to Aachen, everything was as we had left it. There were more soldiers in the city perhaps, but life had not changed. School soon reopened, and the playground in the Kurgarten was as filled with children as ever. Didn't war have the power to touch us at home? Was it just a few battles fought in faraway places?

Father disagreed. "This war will bring more suffering and bloodshed to the world than any before," he warned. He had been in World War I. During the assault on Liège, in the first week of the fighting, a German force had mistaken his platoon for the enemy. Before the error was known, he lay badly wounded. He stubbornly refused to let the surgeons cut off his leg and after ten months, was able to leave the hospital on two legs, but he had to walk with a cane ever after and always felt pain.

So the war had ended quickly for Father. Unfit for combat duty, he was stationed as an army mail inspector in Tilsit, East Prussia, and later in Mönchengladbach. There he met my mother, and both of them often joked about the mysterious ways of God that had brought them together by way of a German mix-up at Liège, two misdirected machine gun bullets and a torn leg, which, in turn, had led to his appointment as officer in charge of military mail censorship in Mother's hometown.

Father had often told us how the people had welcomed the first world war with music and flowers in a burst of misguided patriotism which had slowly given way to sullen gloom as the conflict dragged on to its bloody end. This time, there was no joy at the outbreak of war, not on the steamer from Borkum and not in Aachen. There was only fear and foreboding. But as the victory messages poured in, the church offered thanks to God for the swift triumph of German arms, and a confident mood took hold of my people. I, too, felt proud of being German.

CHAPTER 2

In the early spring of 1940, the city took on a decidedly martial appearance. The streets teemed with soldiers. Three officers were quartered in our house, and best of all, the cooks of one battalion parked their field kitchen in the courtyard behind Father's store. Hermann and I loved to climb all over the shiny two-wheeler with its collapsible stovepipe to which it owed its popular nickname *Gulaschkanone*. We took out the cauldrons, pans, and other utensils stashed away in hidden compartments and dreamed of military life. How romantic it would be to bivouac at nightfall by a rippling stream. Resting around the campfire, the whole company would break into song, and then, silhouetted against the red sunset, the black *Gulaschkanone* would appear on the horizon with a delicious stew or a steaming lentil soup for the tired warriors.

The corporal in charge of the field kitchen listened with undisguised amusement to our chatter. "Well, it isn't quite like that," he said, chuckling without, however, making any effort to correct our fanciful vision of what it meant to be a soldier. We liked him a lot, for he was good-natured and did not mind repolishing his beautiful *Gulaschkanone* each time we had misused it for our gymnastic exercises.

Once, he even let us ride with him to the drill-ground where his battalion was playing war games. We watched him fire up his stove and prepare a savory hot pot. When it was done, he handed us each a mess kit and told us to stand in line with the rest of the soldiers, who treated us little recruits almost as equals. Did we want to march to

Paris with them? Yes, I replied, we would love to, but it all depended on my teacher, Herr Perseke. I wasn't sure he would excuse me from school. They all burst out laughing.

At last, it was our turn to be served by the corporal. He slopped a bountiful portion of the grub into our tins and threw us a hefty piece of tough *Kommissbrot*. Hermann and I devoured it all as if it were the tastiest meal we had ever eaten.

Next morning, I cornered Herr Perseke and tried to get a leave of absence from my class. He flatly refused, insisting that education was far too important to be given up for a *Tour de France*.

A few weeks later, he visited our house to say goodbye to my parents and me. He had been drafted and was about to leave for the army. "But that isn't fair," I shouted, "you wouldn't let me quit school, and now you are doing it yourself!"

Herr Perseke gently stroked my head. "Be glad you are too young to be drafted. I have no desire to go to war and would much rather keep on teaching you."

Mother echoed his unpatriotic remarks. "I give thanks to God every day that no one in my family will have to fight. My sons are still children, and my husband is exempt from active duty thanks to his disability from World War I. War isn't what you think," she said to me, pointing to Father's bad leg, "it's injuries and suffering, death and mourning."

Father served Herr Perseke a cognac and toasted to his safe return. I have no idea whether he did come back alive, but I do know I was sorry to see him go. I never liked the old man who took his place in school.

In late spring, my cousin Karla married one of the officers stationed in our house. I had, of course, noticed their budding romance but paid little heed to it beyond snickering at their foolish behavior. Shortly after the wedding, all army units left Aachen. Squadrons of *Stuka* dive bombers roared overhead toward the western sky. The *Gulaschkanone*, too, rolled off. The nearby Belgian city of Liège, where Father had been wounded in 1914, fell to the *Wehrmacht*. France surrendered. The British were driven from the continent. I began to believe in the infallibility of our Führer and his armed forces, but Father and Mother found no joy in the ever-expanding conflict. Even the steady diet of victory announcements coming from our radio set could not dispel their somber mood.

Karla's husband of a few days never returned from the campaign.

CHAPTER 3

In the winter months, I lost myself in the world of the old Germanic epics where entire nations perish in glorious fulfillment of their destinies. Heroes pledged allegiance to their kings and stooped to treachery to keep their troth. For the sake of honor and vengeance, they sacrificed their lives. And starkly, the bard's lay sings of triumph and defeat, of love and implacable hate, of wild revels, and the convulsions of death.

I also spent many hours reading my volumes of *Der gute Kamerad*, a set of oversize books stuffed with adventures and instructive stories. One of these, I never forgot. A gang of Chinese bandits had fallen upon a train carrying White travelers through the steppes of Central Asia. They were about to rob and kill their panic-stricken victims when the hero, a young German, boldly stepped forward. *"Aleman," he shouted, and again full of strength and pride, "Aleman!"* I am convinced, after all these years that this line is an exact quotation from the story though I must confess to some doubt as to whether the Chinese would really understand the word *Aleman*. At any rate, upon seeing the confident bearing of the young man and especially upon learning of his nationality, they spared the passengers' lives. The mere mention of the fatherland must have struck terror into their hearts, or perhaps they held Germany in such high esteem that they allowed the train to continue on its way.

Naturally, such stirring and uplifting tales swelled my head. Wasn't it wonderful to be German when the single word *Aleman*, even thousands of miles from home, had the power to effect such a miraculous rescue?

In December 1941, the United States entered the war. Well, what difference did it make? The Third Reich was already doing battle against dozens of foes, so why should one more matter? Father listened with a pained expression, yet patiently, to his nine-year-old son's astute observations. Then he simply asked me to fetch the atlas. He opened it on a double page with a map of the world. "Show me the Soviet Union and the United States," he said. "Now, where is Germany?" I thought I knew geography. Finding America and Russia was easy, but it took me a while to locate the tiny area called Germany, squeezed into insignificance between the enormous mass of the giants on its right and left.

I was taken aback. How could this map reduce my country to such a small speck when elsewhere in this same atlas it filled a whole page just like America and Russia? Father gave me a brief nonpolitical lesson on geography and scale. By the time he was done, he had sowed the first seeds of doubt in my mind.

CHAPTER 4

After Easter 1942, when the new school year started, all my classmates were in the *Hitler-Jugend* or rather in its subdivision for younger boys, the *Deutsches Jungvolk*. Membership in this organization was made compulsory for all ten- to fourteen-year-olds in 1939. Actually, few of us could wait for the day we would be entitled to wear the *Jungvolk's* resplendent uniform. I was jealous to see my friends strut through the streets in their trappings of black shorts, brown shirt, black scarf fastened around the neck with a leather knot, and their smart caps. But most of all, I lusted after the broad sword belt with its shiny buckle and the sheath knife dangling from its side. I felt like a plucked cock among crowing roosters of iridescent plumage. Though still four months short of my tenth birthday, I was determined to join the *Jungvolk* and thus rectify my nakedness at once.

They took me in. Proudly I pledged my allegiance: "In the presence of this blood banner, which represents our Führer, I swear to devote all my powers and energies to the savior of our country, Adolf Hitler. I am willing to give up my life for him, so help me God."

The leader administering the oath concluded the solemn ceremony with a brief sermon. "Only the strong in mind and body can hope to be prepared for the ultimate test of manhood, the readiness to sacrifice oneself, unflinchingly, for a noble cause. Your initiation into the *Jungvolk* is the first step in your education for service to the fatherland. Today, you are becoming part of a great movement. I know you will not dishonor it."

Every week, we were drilled in a barrack-square and taught to march in rank and file. We pushed ourselves to the limits of endurance: running, marching, jumping, marching, putting the shot, marching, hurling the *Schleuderball*, marching. And to make sure our minds would not be neglected, there were frequent orations by visiting speakers to enlighten us on some aspect of the Führer's thought. *Mens sana in corpore sano.*

I learned that war was a glorious test of will from which the strong emerge triumphant. I learned that the Germanic race was the salt of the earth, a kind of chosen people destined to rule the world. I learned that our racial heritage was our most precious possession, an immaculate pearl we must not throw to the swine.

Sometimes we were marched into the concert hall of the *Altes Kurhaus* to listen to music, the *glory of German civilization*. For these occasions, boys and girls were especially spruced up: uniforms spotless and shoes, belts, and buckles shiny. While many of my comrades had great difficulty hiding their boredom, I thoroughly enjoyed Wagner's *Siegfried Idyll*, his ouverture to *Die Meistersinger*, or Beethoven's *Fifth Symphony*. Can it be that I owe my lifelong love of music to these early sessions of compulsory culture?

Often, the *Jungvolk* meetings took place on Sunday mornings to keep us from going to mass, but the church—accommodating as always—held additional services on Saturdays and Sunday nights. Thus, I was able to combine my secular and religious duties, to render unto Caesar the things which are Caesar's and to God the things which are God's.

At that time I had no idea what a Jew was. I must have dozed through the Scripture readings and sermons in church, for I had never heard the word mentioned there. In fact, I could remember hearing about Jews only once before in my life. That was in November 1938, after the infamous *Kristallnacht*. One morning, on my way to school, I had found many stores vandalized, doors and windows smashed to pieces. To my excited questions, the teacher, Herr Perseke, merely answered that all these stores belonged to the Jews. When I asked why the police had not arrested the thugs responsible for the destruction, he smiled sadly and added, "But the looting was carried out by order of the government."

In my naive eyes, the government stood for law and order. If it unleashed its wrath against them, surely the Jews had committed some horrible deeds and deserved to be punished. A strange association was born in my mind: *Jew* became simply a synonym for evildoer.

But the Jungvolk lectures did not quite square with that notion. The more I listened, the more convinced I became that Jews were not just ordinary outlaws. Beneath that name lurked something dark, unclean, and vaguely decadent yet at the same time something threatening and all-pervasive.

I wanted to know more about these mysterious Jews. Since the tone of final authority with which our speakers delivered themselves of their *truth* did not encourage questions, I turned to my parents. Mother insisted, to my utter amazement, that Jesus, Mary, and the apostles had all been Jews. Father explained the Nazi racial laws to me. "Suppose I take seven glasses of apple juice and mix them with one glass of water. Then suppose I take one glass of apple juice and mix it with seven glass of water. Which drink would you choose?"

"The first one, of course."

"Why?"

"Because it's almost pure apple juice, whereas the second pitcher is mostly water."

"Exactly," said Father. "We Germans are supposed to be the superior race, but if only one of your great grandparents had been Jewish, then you would be an outcast in your own country. Now if one-part Jewish blood can get the better of seven parts German blood, doesn't it follow that the Jews are the superior and we the inferior race?"

Father left me to ponder this rhetorical question. I was shattered by what I had learned in the past hour. Was my faith in the Führer and his spokesmen just a foolish delusion? I could not believe that. And yet I trusted my parents and felt deep down they were right.

It was becoming more difficult every day to reconcile these two sources of truth in my life. I resolved to keep the worlds of family and Führer separate henceforth, like matter and antimatter, which upon contact would annihilate each other. Though no one had told me so, I sensed it would be dangerous to mention my parents' ideas outside the home.

CHAPTER 5

To perform such a mental balancing act was no easy matter. Through my double vision, the world appeared in a blurred, confused outline. It was as if a tightrope walker suddenly saw *two* vibrating wires stretched beneath him, knowing there was really only one, unsure where to place his feet.

Naturally, such strain did not aid my concentration. My mind was absent from school, and I very nearly failed to be promoted to the second grade of my gymnasium. It happened that at the end of a period, I might not even remember whether I had sat through a math or a history class.

The war cast its lengthening shadows over all aspects of life, and school was no exception. Many venerable retired schoolmasters had been called back into service to replace the younger teachers who were manning the Atlantic Wall or fighting somewhere in the vastness of Russia or under the scorching sun of North Africa. Some of these old men had either developed peculiar quirks with advancing years or perhaps simply conserved the methods of another age. My math teacher was an especially unforgettable character. He delighted in springing a surprising question on some unsuspecting student and, brandishing a wet eraser, was ever ready to hurl it with deadly accuracy, born of a lifetime's experience, in the boy's face if his answer was too long in coming. Of course, most of us were too preoccupied with evading the wet missile to be able to reason out a mathematical problem. By such and similar means, he even succeeded, sometimes, in making me realize I was in school and not alone in my room, brooding about my conflicting thoughts and emotions. Still, I did not learn much from him, but to this day, I retain a certain affection mixed with sadness when I think of him. His life had been devoted passionately to the futile effort to reform the German number system. "We should not say *einundzwanzig, zweiundzwanzig,* but *zwanzig und eins, zwanzig und zwei,*" he repeated, endlessly, lamenting the blindness of the powers that be which had failed to see the brilliance and force of his *revolutionary idea,* as he referred to his rather simple-minded notion.

Decidedly, the quality of instruction was not raised by turning the schools over to the likes of this pleasant, superannuated pensioner. As for me, I managed to advance to the next class, and as I became more adept at performing my mental balancing act, my scholastic achievements returned to their former high level.

CHAPTER 6

In the early morning hours of August 1942, more than a thousand boys, smartly attired in their uniforms and loaded down with bulky rucksacks, assembled on the Kaiserplatz. Soon, we lined up in marching formation, impatient to set out for Mausbach where we were to spend three weeks in a *Jungvolk* camp. But first, we would have a chance to show off to our admiring parents the incredible precision and finely honed marching skills we had acquired in those endless drills on the barrack grounds. Sharp commands traveled up and down the columns until, at the exact moment, perfectly synchronized, all thousand of us briskly stepped forward bursting into song: *"Es zittern die morschen Knochen der Welt vor dem grossen Krieg."* ("The rotten bones of the world tremble before the great war.")

Five hours later, a bedraggled troupe, tired, thirsty, and covered with dust, arrived at Mausbach. To my wayworn legs, the camp gates with their legend *Führer, Volk, und Vaterland* seemed like the gates of paradise promising rest to the weary. Our spirits revived, and goaded on by our leaders, who were intent on making a good impression on the all-powerful camp Commander, we mustered what strength we still had and proudly marched onto the campgrounds singing: *"Heute gehört uns Deutschland und morgen die ganze Welt."* ("Today Germany is ours, tomorrow the whole world.") Actually, I was ready to trade the world for a comfortable bed to rest my aching back and feet, just as Esau sold his birthright for a mess of pottage.

I was a big eater and soon discovered I could get two extra pieces of bread by volunteering for guard duty. As keeper of the gate, I had to do one two-hour stint during the day and another one at night, checking everyone who went in and out of camp.

It was my turn to stand guard the night the *Jungvolk* put on a show for the people of the surrounding towns. Countless times, I raised and lowered the gate for the many visitors, cursing my ill-luck which caused me to miss all the fun. A little later, when it started to rain, I sat down in the sentry box for a moment. Presently, I dozed off and fell into a happy dream of being promoted from ordinary *Pimpf to Hordenführer*, which would entitle me to wear a red and white ribbon on my breast. Suddenly I was jolted by a strong hand and heard a booming voice demand, "How dare you betray *Führer, Volk, und Vaterland* by sleeping while on guard duty." I froze to attention in a respectful salute, for I realized from the insignia of rank dangling before my incredulous eyes that this awesome stranger was none other than the *Oberbannführer*, a dignitary I saw in my mind as sitting on the right-hand side of the Führer himself. There had been rumors this high official, busy though he was with great matters of state, might condescend to honor our show with his exalted presence. And here he was in the flesh, *a deus ex machina*, who had stepped from his limousine almost two hours late, but just in time for the end of the play. There he stood dripping in the rain outside my sentry box, putting an end to my dreams of promotion. "Your dereliction of duty will have consequences," he said and climbed back into his car as I hastened to raise and lower the boom.

There were consequences, foul and noxious. Next morning, the camp commander summoned me to his office and sternly rebuked me for my flagrant transgression of the night before. "You'll atone for this," he announced. "Go and join the penal detachment of miscreants behind the north barracks. They are on latrine duty, emptying the cesspool. I order you to work with them."

An aide handed me a shovel. My mission was to cleanse both self and cesspool. As I approached the open pit, I saw my companions in misfortune already started on their redeeming labor, splattered with the putrid filth excreted by the *HitlerJugend* Camp. The onslaught of the malodorous effluvium made my stomach turn and my knees buckle. I knew I would not be able to go through with it.

Quickly I dropped my shovel, turned on my heels, and left the scene without a word of explanation. I would sooner face a firing squad than do the commander's bidding. Thus, at the age of ten, I performed my first overt act of resistance to the Third Reich, though, alas, I must give credit for it to my sensitive nose rather than to my convictions. The spirit had been willing, but the flesh was weak.

I awaited my fate with resignation. Day after day went by and nothing happened. At last, it dawned on me that in the person of the penal detachment's leader I had come face-to-face with the human side of Nazism. He lived a block from us in Aachen. So we knew each other by sight; perhaps, he had sensed my quiet admiration. No doubt he had noticed my extreme revulsion at the edge of the pit and taken pity on me instead of reporting me to the authorities. A week later, he said jokingly, as we met by chance near the latrine, "I see you don't like to poke your nose into everything. Well, this time you had a good nose, *eine feine Nase*, for what you could get away with." A year later, he was buried beneath the rubble of his house, a victim of one of the air raids on our town.

CHAPTER 7

Three weeks of Mausbach had succeeded in reinfecting my susceptible mind with the ideas of faith in the Führer, service to the fatherland, and triumph through war. So when I got word that our region had chosen me to attend the *Adolf Hitler Schule,* I swelled with pride. I would be one of the elite, trained in this special school for future leaders of Reich and Party. The unpardonable offense of sleeping through guard duty had been forgiven, and a godsent opportunity had come my way, raising me to the ranks of the elect. Scarcely able to contain my rapture, I saw myself in my dreams as a successor to the Führer's throne or at least as one of the great paladins of his court.

A delegation of notables had come to our house to announce the honor that has befallen me. Each one of them seemed to me a radiant angel of annunciation bearing glad tidings. They disappeared behind the closed doors of our living room with my parents who look pained, as if in the throes of a difficult decision. Why are they staying so long? What are they talking about all this time?

Impatiently, I paced up and down the hallway. They must be discussing my life away from home. At this very moment, perhaps, they were fixing the date of my departure. Suddenly the door was flung open. The red-faced visitors, more like avenging angels now, stomped out with a curt *"Heil Hitler."* Father bowed stiffly. Mother looked positively happy. She clasped me in her arms and said amid tears of joy, "You don't have to leave us. Father told them he will not let you go."

I was stunned, though not really taken unawares. I protested, "But this is the chance of a lifetime—"

Mother was still holding me tightly. "God knows what sick ideas they would have stuffed into your head at that school. Besides, your father and I need you and want you here with us."

CHAPTER 8

Time heals many wounds. I knew my heart was with my parents and soon began to feel actually relieved at having stayed at home. The loss of the *Adolf Hitler Schule* was, after all, not quite the same thing as paradise lost. I didn't need that school to prove myself. There was challenge enough for me right here in my own gymnasium, trying to perfect my skill at dodging the math teacher's wet erasers.

But though I had lowered my sights a little, I had not given up all ambition. If I could no longer aspire to a place in the sun near the Führer himself, I could at least advance to *Hordenführer*. To prepare the way for this modest first step up the ladder of success, I decided to make an all-out effort to collect used paper for recycling into the war economy. When the results were announced to all the students lined up in the schoolyard, I had come in first. A local party leader praised my devotion to the cause. The director presented me with a copy of *Mein Kampf*, bound in black like the Bible. I must confess I was somewhat disappointed with my prize. What I really wanted to win was a paint box. Besides, I knew that, thanks to the government's largesse, I would get another one of these ponderous tomes as a wedding gift, and I felt quite capable of postponing my reading pleasure till then. Today, I cannot help smiling at the irony that all my paper was probably ground to pulp only to be reprocessed into still more copies of the Führer's Holy Writ.

The whole gathering started singing our two national anthems—the traditional *Deutschlandlied* to the music of Joseph Haydn and the *Horst-Wessel-Lied*, added by the NSDAP (the *Nationalsozialistische*

Deutsche Arbeiterpartei, i.e., the Nazi Party). As an unintended result of the Jungvolk's compulsory culture sessions, my musical taste was by now sufficiently developed to make me detest the exceedingly primitive melody of that second song. Its words, with their convoluted syntax, never did make sense to me either: *"Kameraden, die Rotfront und Reaktion erschossen..."* Comrades who shot red front and reaction? Comrades whom red front and reaction shot? What was red front and reaction anyway? I always rattled off the text by rote like the Latin responses in church.

The strains of the national anthems caused me to spring to attention like a jumping jack. I imagined all eyes upon me as I stood exposed in the center of the schoolyard, my right arm extended in the Hitler salute. Thank God I had enough strength now to hold it up to the very end! Until recently, the interminable ritual of singing through two anthems had invariably brought on an embarrassing muscle spasm which made my arm waver and drop, forcing me to jerk it back up repeatedly. My *mens* might not be *sana*, but at least the Jungvolk's physical fitness training had given me a *corpus sanum*.

Next, I scored a big success in this year's *Winterhilfe*, a fund-raising drive to purchase warm clothes for the troops facing another Russian winter. By dint of long hours in the streets of Aachen and the relentless pursuit of every passerby with my collecting box, I managed to turn in a large sum of money. Father, too, tossed in a few coins. "Those poor soldiers will be lucky to get out of Russia alive," he said. He talked to me about the German offensives of the previous two summers, about Stalingrad and the army's heavy losses, its failure to gain any ground this year, and its present exhaustion. On a map, he pointed out the large-scale retreat all along the Eastern front. Finally, he took *Mein Kampf* off my bookshelf, opened it, and read, "Germany will either be a world power, or there will be no Germany." He paused for a moment and then added, "May God grant that Hitler is wrong on both counts. I cannot hope that we will win the war and be a world power, but I pray Germany will not perish either."

Having collected high marks, both as a paper and money collector, I was in a good position to try out for promotion in the *Jungvolk*.

I had already met all athletic standards—only an intelligence test stood between me and the rank of *Hordenführer*. I was supremely confident I could readily surpass the minimal mental requirements needed for advancement in the *Jungvolk* as I sat down for the examination. The hardest question came first: "What is the Führer's date of birth?" I had no idea. Even today, I don't know anybody's birthday except my own. Fortunately, my wife is sensible enough not to draw any negative conclusions about my fitness as a husband from this defect of memory. The humorless examiners, however, looked upon the blank I had left after question number one as a sort of lèse-majesté. In vain, I protested that the Führer's birthday had always been very dear to me—it meant an extra school holiday. My inability to put down April 20, 1889, doomed me to remain a simple *Pimpf*.

CHAPTER 9

The sound of sirens had become as familiar to us as our own voices. A constant tone marked every few seconds by a drop in pitch was the warning signal—a rapid, wavelike rise and fall meant full alarm and a long, steady sound maintained for a whole minute proclaimed the all clear. It was by now clear to all that Göring's air force was more invisible than invincible despite the corpulent Reichsmarschall's earlier boasts that no enemy plane would be allowed to violate the German skies. What little defense there still was against the perpetual air raids came from antiaircraft fire. Hermann and I often scurried to the site of a crash to pick up pieces of scrap from a downed American or British plane. An instrument from the panel would be a prize find for our collection.

My hometown is the westernmost city in Germany. From the cathedral, you could walk in less than an hour to Belgium or the Netherlands. The howl of full alarm, night after night, made me think that Aachen was the place where all Allied planes crossed the border with their deadly cargo. Usually the drone of the engines, riddled by the sound of flak, lasted only for a few minutes as the bombing squadrons headed elsewhere. But when the target was Aachen, the sky burst open, hurling fearsome bolts of thunder and lightning upon us. The day of doom seemed at hand. These raids were aptly called *Terrorangriffe* (terror attacks) in newspapers and on radio broadcasts.

At last, an attack would be over. Like frightened moles, we emerged from our underground hideouts and found another part of the city gone. Sometimes, the devastation had struck in a random pattern. At other times, the bombs had carved out a swath of destruction which we described as a *bomb carpet* because it looked from the nearby hills as if a rug had been unrolled across the town, flattening everything beneath it.

We tried to feel safe in our damp and musty basement. Our house, a former hotel, extensively remodeled by my grandfather, had four solid floors. So we convinced ourselves that any bomb would lose most of its force before reaching the thick cellar vaults. Besides, a narrow tunnel had been burrowed through the wall into the neighbor's basement. It was sealed with a single layer of brick, easy to open with a few blows of the sledgehammer. These subterranean interconnections extended the length of the street giving us an escape hatch should we be buried under heaps of rubble.

It was only when I could not make it back home before the first explosions ripped the air that I ever set foot in one of the bombproof concrete shelters the government had put up throughout the city. Inside, thousands of people crouched on wooden benches or huddled against the walls. It was hot and stifling in these bunkers because they lacked adequate ventilation. But worst of all was the palpable angst that filled the atmosphere: the cold sweat, the fingering and reciting of rosaries, the cursing, the crying of children, the chattering of teeth, the incessant babbling of some, and the silence of haunted faces with unsteady, flickering eyes. The fear was contagious, and I always felt relieved when the steel doors swung open to let me out.

I much preferred sitting on my straw mattress in the narrow, vaulted corridor of our own basement. There was at least the comfort that our whole family was together. With us were my uncle and aunt and the Kretens, who rented an apartment on the fourth floor. Each of us had a suitcase or two containing a few possessions which we meant to carry with us if the house should be destroyed.

My sister Marita had gone to Heringsdorf to spend a month in a children's home. In her letters, she marveled at the quiet and peacefulness of Pomerania. There had not been a single alarm in her first two weeks on the Baltic coast. How I wished we could all be there!

On the night of July 14, 1943, one of the worst *Terrorangriffe* on my city took place. Our house, too, was hit by incendiary bombs. I wanted to help put out the fire, but Father forbade me to leave the cellar. Why did he treat me like a child though I was nearly eleven years old and knew exactly what to do? I knew where the sandbags were kept. I knew where to find the water buckets and the grappling hooks, and I could run up to the attic in a minute to tear down the burning rafters.

Father couldn't move fast. He had to climb the stairs with a cane because of the injury to his leg. I feared for him as he battled the blaze without me. At last, he returned looking grimy and exhausted. He couldn't save the house. Phosphorous bombs had lit it in a dozen places.

Herr Kreten suddenly remembered he had left eighty Reichsmarks on his desk. He insisted upon rushing up to recover the money. With difficulty, he was restrained from risking his life in the conflagration. Already the walls and roof were caving in.

The air raid was over. Father tried to go back up to see if it was safe for us to leave, but the wreckage caused by explosions had blocked the way out. We knocked down the partition to the neighbor's basement, grabbed our suitcases, and wrapped ourselves in wet blankets. We surfaced into the street. A blaze of heat hit us.

Mother and I hurried through the raging inferno up toward the Salvatorberg. We stopped and looked back. The whole city was a lake of fire—the sky, dense smoke, and leaping flames. Bursts of sparks shot up from tumbling buildings. Everywhere dark shadow figures, flushed from their burrows, slipped through the flames to safety. Like Sodom and Gomorrah, Aachen was being consumed by fire and brimstone—a scene from hell, yet strangely beautiful.

It was about four kilometers to our relatives' villa in Laurensberg. I could hardly lift the suitcases, but I knew Mother's were even heavier than mine. I clenched my fists and hung on to my bags.

Near Laurensberg, my older cousin Hans-Günter spotted us. He was directing the stream of refugees from the city. Has he seen Father and Hermann? No, they had not come this way.

Mother and I were certain they had escaped from the cellar. But where could they be? Hours went by, and we still did not know their fate. At last, Hermann arrived. He was welcomed with more joy than the long-lost prodigal son. We pounced on him with frantic questions. "Yes, Father is all right. He is in Herr Münzer's, the orthopaedist, house. Father couldn't see and had trouble breathing. Herr Münzer saw us groping our way through the street and took us in. He has called a physician who says the blindness and coughing are caused by smoke. The doctor has given Father some salve and eye patches. He'll be better in a day or two."

Father had told Hermann to hurry on to Laurensberg to join us. When he got to Veltmanplatz, he felt tired and lay down on a bench for a moment. He was awakened by a bomb disposal squad which had started working on a *Blindgänger* (dud) right beside the bench and ordered him to leave at once. So here he was, a little late, but well-rested, having refreshed himself with a nap practically on top of an unexploded bomb.

Mother sent me to the post office with a message for a telegram to Heringsdorf: "We are all alive." She and HansGünter set out for Aachen to get Father.

CHAPTER 10

Our worldly belongings had shrunk to the contents of six suitcases of varying size. My parents must have felt despair at having lost in one brief moment the fruits of their lives' labor. But with what courage and strength they bore their lot, uncomplaining, without bitterness, never showing a trace of despondency to us.

The day of our arrival in Laurensberg, Mother took a book of poems from Aunt Else's shelf and read from Schiller's poem *Das Lied von der Glocke* ("The Song of the Bell").

...

Beneficent the might of flame
If watched by man, by him made tame;
For to this heavenly power he owes
All his creative genius knows.
Yet terrible this heavenly fire
If once it bursts its chains in ire
And leaps along its self-made path
Free Nature's daughter, full of wrath!

Woe, if it casts off its chains,
And, without resistance growing,
Through the crowded streets and lanes
Spreads the blaze, all fiercely glowing!
For the elements still hate
All that human hands create.

...
Hear the bell foreboding harm!
Fire alarm!
Blood-red, lo,
Is the sky;
But 'tis not the day's clear glow,
Flickering high.
Tumult in the street,
Smoke and heat!
High the fiery column glows,
Through the streets' far stretching rows
On with lightning speed it goes.
Hot, as from an oven's womb,
Burns the air, while beams consume;
Windows rattle, pillars fall,
Children wail and mothers call.
Beasts are groaning,
Underneath the ruins moaning.
All their safety seek in flight,
Day-clear lighted is the night.
Through the hands' extended chain
Flies the bucket on amain;
Floods of water, high arched, spurting
Howling comes the storm, low skirting,
Roaring in the fire's pursuit.
Crackling mid the withered fruit
In the lofts it searches after
Every dried-up beam and rafter,
And, as if earth's heavy weight
Seeking in its flight to bear,
It mounts, like a giant great,
Wildly through the realms of air.
Man now loses hope at length,
Yielding to immortal strength,
Idly and with wondering gaze,
The wreckage of his works surveys.

Burnt to ashes is the stead,
Now the wild storm's rough-hewn bed.
In the deserted windows loom
Horror, desolation, gloom,
And the clouds that dark the sky
Look in from high.
One last lingering look man throws
On the barren grave
Of all that Fortune gave,
Then, as a pilgrim, onward goes.
Whate'er the wrath of fire has shorn,
One comfort sweet is yet remaining:
He counts his loved ones, uncomplaining,
For see! no one from him is torn.

. . .

Mother stopped here, tears in her eyes. She put her arms around Hermann and me and repeated in a whisper, "No one from us is torn."

Later, Father told us he had seen a fire engine waiting in the Minoritenstrasse across from our house while he was trying to put out the flames. When he had asked the men for help, they had refused, citing strict orders to protect only the nearby Cathedral and Rathaus. Their blind, fanatical obedience to instructions in the face of an urgent job to be done had enraged my father.

At first, I shared his feelings, for we were homeless. And I had lost all my possessions: bicycle, gramophone, collection of scrap metal from downed planes, and my books, including the still unread copy of *Mein Kampf*, now reduced to ashes. But gradually, I changed my mind. As I walked through my ruined city, I sometimes had trouble recognizing where I was. Familiar landmarks had disappeared. Entire streets lay in waste with blackened facades rising from the rubble. The Couven Museum, the theater, one of the medieval city gates, many churches, and the Elisenbrunnen were either destroyed or badly damaged, but there, right in the heart of Aachen, still stood the Chapel Palatine with its soaring Gothic choir and the town hall built on the remnants of Charlemagne's palace. These are the soul of Aachen and what does it profit a city to save its ordinary houses if it loses its soul?

The Cathedral suffered serious damage during the war but survived the bombardments. The Rathaus, though close to collapse, was eventually restored and saved. In the end two thirds of Aachen lay in ruins. The city has long since risen from its ashes, yet how much poorer it would be without its ancient soul. Yes, the firemen had been right to let our house burn down. Moreover, their hands-off attitude and the Allied bombs had quite possibly spared the Party the trouble of having to decide whether to close my father's business. Would his flat refusal to let me go to the *Adolf Hitler Schule* have brought on this form of retaliation if the premises had not been shut down by a *force majeure?* We shall never know.

CHAPTER 11

In church, I had heard the *"Gebet für den Führer"* (Prayer for the Führer), yet my parents told me that by order of that same Führer, monasteries had been closed down and confiscated, the diocesan newspaper prohibited, and Canon Jansen of the Cathedral chapter arrested. In school, we read the glorious epics of our Germanic forbears. We learned how a small band of brave men, yes even a single hero, can turn the tide of battle and prevail over any number of foes if only he can elude the traitor's snares. In the *Jungvolk*, the *Stammführer* proudly assured us the fatherland would still need all our courage and devotion when we were men. "The Führer and his army will soon win this war, but the world is forever conspiring to bring down the pure and strong. We, too, will have a chance to show our mettle, to dedicate ourselves to Führer, Volk, and Vaterland."

To my timid question how it was possible for the enemy to devastate our cities with impunity, he replied that this was proof of treachery and cowardice. "They don't dare face our soldiers on the battlefield, so they drop their bombs in the darkness of night, hoping to break our will to resist. But they will never succeed. Victory will be ours. The enemy must pay for his crimes."

I was convinced. I loved my city and hated all who were destroying it. Just in this latest air raid, they had dropped over one hundred thirty thousand incendiary and phosphorous bombs on Aachen besides hundreds of mines and high-explosive bombs. If only I were old enough to join the students of the upper grades who were manning the flak batteries around Aachen as *Luftwaffenhelfer* (air force helpers). Here I was, still a boy warming a school bench, wasting my time on Pythagoras and irregular verbs, while *they* were men defending their country. Why hadn't my parents given birth to me a few years earlier? How I would love to shoot down a plane!

My math teacher reminded me that a thorough knowledge of geometry and arithmetic was required to calculate the correct path of a shell moving toward an object in flight. I felt ready to make *any* sacrifice asked of me to play my part in this great struggle against the rest of the world, even if it meant I had to master the most unfathomable mysteries of mathematics, and I delighted the venerable schoolmaster by the prodigious feats of study I devoted to a subject hitherto slighted by me.

There was one sacrifice, however, I had been unwilling to make. For Christmas of 1940, my parents had given me a pair of skis. Shortly thereafter, the army had requisitioned all skis for the *Gebirgsjäger* (mountain troops) in Norway. Having used them only a few times on the tobogganing run in the Stadtgarten, I could not bring myself to part with them and carefully hid them in the attic.

This past winter, I had persuaded the driver of my father's delivery van to take the skis to a friend's place in a remote rural section of Laurensberg. Behind his house, there was a sloping meadow, shielded from view, and there we had indulged in the forbidden pleasures of skiing though I had never been able to rid myself of a guilty conscience for my selfish refusal to turn the skis over to the *Gebirgsjäger*. Now, filled with a fresh zeal to serve my country, I felt actually relieved that the incriminating boards had gone up in flames in the latest air raid.

I spouted off some of my new wisdom to my parents as if it were my own. "They are afraid to fight our soldiers," I announced, "that's why these cowards drop bombs on our cities. But we are going to show them when we win this war."

Mother gently said it was hard to believe in victory any longer. People had to hand over their copper pots to feed the famished war industry. Last year already church bells and bronze monuments had been melted down. "And how can you win a war with the *Hühnerdieb* and the *Fischpüddelchen?*" she asked ironically, referring to the city's popular fountain sculptures of a chicken thief and a naked boy with waterspewing fishes under his arms.

Then Father continued in a more serious vein. "You say the enemy is too cowardly to face our *Wehrmacht*. Have you already forgotten what happened at Stalingrad? Our men fought bravely, but so did the Russians. And there are many more of them than of us."

I thought back to the disaster that had befallen the German army in Russia. Week after week, our ears were glued to our radio sets listening to the latest *Sondermeldungen* (special announcements) about the course of the epic battle. Earlier in the war, such special announcements were broadcast to the accompaniment of fanfares and trumpets to make known a great victory. This time, the tone soon changed from confident anticipation of triumph to desperate insistence that German troops would never surrender but fight on to the last drop of blood. The final bulletin came hardly as a surprise to anyone. For days, we had all known that the end was drawing near.

In the next twenty-four hours, all radio stations played funeral music interrupted only by an occasional tribute to the fallen heroes or a half-hearted attempt to make us believe that their sacrifice was the seed from which the *Endsieg* (final victory) would spring.

Though I was not yet eleven years old, I could feel how the mood of the people changed at that time. Even the *Stammführer* and our most rabid teacher seemed like deflated balloons, lacking the buoyancy to launch into one of their familiar flights of grandiloquent optimism. To give a badly needed lift both to its forlorn disciples and to the population in general, the regime started one of the greatest propaganda actions ever seen.

The climax of this campaign was Goebbels's masterful speech in the Berlin Sportpalast. I remember well watching it in the *Wochenschau* (newsreel) of a local movie house. The "Reichsminister for National Enlightenment and Propaganda" hypnotized his listeners into a frenzy of delirious passion and flinging his questions into the crowd received back a chorus of fanatic replies.

"Are you ready to stand, with the Führer, like a phalanx behind the fighting *Wehrmacht* and to continue the struggle with ferocious and unflinching determination through all trials of fate until victory is in our hands?"

"We are ready."

"Do you believe in total war?"

"We believe."

"Are you ready to follow the Führer, no matter what personal sacrifices he may demand, to save the world from the Bolshevik menace and the imperialist-capitalist conspiracy?"

"Führer command, we obey."

"Are you determined, if the Führer so orders, to work ten, twelve, and if necessary, fourteen and sixteen hours a day?"

"Führer command, we obey."

To my surprise, I heard myself shouting with many others in the theater. Yes, I would do my part and study my math lessons with untiring zeal so that I would be ready to become a *Luftwaffenhelfer* when the Führer would call me.

"Do you agree that racketeers and profiteers and all those whose selfishness undermines the war effort shall lose their heads?"

"We do."

This time, I remained silent, dumbfounded at the thought that I might be beheaded for the crime of having kept my skis for myself.

Goebbels ended with a jubilant exhortation: *"Nun Volk, steh' auf, und Sturm brich los!"* (Nation arise and burst forth like a storm!)

Still in a daze as I left the theater, I ran into a wall covered with new posters. They showed the craggy face of a soldier of rocklike, almost otherworldly strength. Below him stood a *Hitler-Jugend* boy, face lifted in a worshipful gaze, cap in one hand, the other placed on his heart. And at the bottom the words: "Stalingrad—undying model for the fighting spirit!" I felt as if that boy were I, and I, too, pledged undying allegiance in my heart to the Führer and his fallen heroes.

But the propaganda minister's rousing speech had not produced any effect on my parents. With the patience of Job, they tried to disabuse me of my delusions. Father loved his country and could not wish for its defeat but neither could he hope for victory. "We don't want total war," he said, "for that means putting all our energies, all our strength, and all our efforts into the service of death and destruction. What we need is total peace." And he proceeded to explain that regardless of his wishes, the war would be lost. The momentum was with the Allies. Their superior numbers and industrial potential would grind down our resistance. "The sooner it happens, the better, to spare the world unnecessary bloodshed and devastation."

Father had joined the Nazi Party in 1932, the year before Hitler came to power. He had been disappointed by the failures of the Weimar Republic, by what seemed to him indecision and confusion in the face of economic and social chaos. Briefly he had been taken in by the Nazi's promises but soon realized how empty they were. He never quit the Party, worried perhaps that such an act of open repudiation of the Third Reich would bring on retaliation against him and his family. His membership, however, remained entirely passive, limited to the payment of his annual dues, until the local *Ortsgruppenführer* told him to volunteer for a more active duty. Father chose to visit wounded soldiers, those recuperating in the hospitals of our area and those so badly maimed they would never see action again. As a former officer, himself injured in World War I, he felt he could fulfill that duty without hypocrisy or a false show of devotion to a cause he no longer believed in.

Father talked to me about the men he had seen, their unspeakable suffering, and the stories they had told him about conditions on the increasingly desperate Eastern front. Then he quoted from Goebbels's speech and the Sermon on the Mount. "'Do you believe in total war?' 'Blessed are the peacemakers; for they shall be called the children of God.' Now choose for yourself who is right," he concluded, "Goebbels or Jesus."

Impressionable as I was, I continued to swing back and forth between the two worlds of family and Führer. Mass rallies with thousands of marchers and flags and uniforms and patriotic speeches cast a hypnotic spell over me. I felt like an organic part of *one* great body, purposefully moving to *one* great will. But in the many intimate talks with my parents, I became a whole person, not just a cog in a giant machine. I thought for myself, asked questions, listened, argued, and felt free. And though I don't remember exactly when I began to see the light, I do know that before a year or two had passed, Father and Mother had converted me from a blind believer to a watchful doubter. Never again would I fall prey to an ideology, never again accept any idea nor even a simple story without testing it in the crucible of critical reasoning. It was, of course, a change for the better, yet it was also a loss. Perhaps, it marked the end of my real childhood when I was not yet thirteen years old. Oh, I did many childish things thereafter, but that open, unquestioning, innocent, childlike belief was forever gone from my life.

CHAPTER 12

Aunt Else's and Uncle Willy's house in Laurensberg looked like an island of peace after the bombed-out city. There was a little garden around the villa with flowers, fruit trees, and a goldfish pool with a fountain. Beyond lay the fields of a neighboring farmer, and across the country road, we could see a wooded park enclosed by a high iron fence. Somewhere inside, but hardly visible in the summer when the foliage was dense, stood a stately old mansion.

All five of us moved in with our relatives, determined to carry on our lives as best we could. Surely, here we were safe. No stray bomb could possibly hit this secluded house sitting amid fields and woods.

My parents decided to enroll Hermann and me in the gymnasium at Herzogenrath. This was farther away than Aachen, but since many schools there, including our own, had been destroyed, the remaining ones suffered from serious overcrowding. Moreover, it seemed less dangerous to travel to a small town north of Laurensberg than to commute into the threatened city which had already endured over three hundred fifty air raid alarms by the fall of 1943.

Mother took my brother and me to the director's office to ask if he would accept us. "Good morning," she said amiably, only to be rebuffed by a very curt, "Heil Hitler! What do you want?" I hastened to mollify the all-important personage with a snappy rendition of the *Deutsche Gruss* (German greeting; i.e., Heil Hitler), and Hermann chimed in, smartly clicking his heels at the same time. The director, appeased by this display of good conduct, apparently concluded that

Mother's lax manners had not yet infected her boys. Soon he relented and agreed to admit us to his school.

On the way back, Mother laughed, "You saved the day. I had quite forgotten that this type of functionary thinks it an insult to be greeted in the good old way. *Guten Tag* is offensive to them while *Heil Hitler* is music to their ears." And she added the Director would really be annoyed if he ever spent a vacation on the Tegernsee, a lake in Bavaria, as we had done in the summer of 1942, for there people still insisted on the traditional *Grüss Gott* (greetings in the name of God) as a form of salutation.

The next academic year had to be counted as a total loss for me, but neither my new gymnasium nor I were to blame for this. After all, I spent considerably more time in the streetcars than in the classroom.

We had received an elaborate set of instructions regulating our daily ride from Laurensberg to Herzogenrath. First, unless the sirens had given the all-clear signal, we were to stay at home. Second, there would be no need to leave for school after twelve o'clock noon since classes ended at 1:30 p.m. Third, if we were already on the way when the warning signal sounded, we should either proceed to the gymnasium or return home depending on whether we had passed the midpoint of our trip. Finally, in case of full alarm, we should at once get off the streetcar and go to the nearest air raid shelter.

These rules, especially the third one, which we commuters interpreted in a very liberal fashion, practically guaranteed that we would miss most of our classes. We were forever shuttling back and forth between Laurensberg and the school, for if we heard any warning siren, no matter how faint or far away, we would jump off our streetcar and hop on the next one going in the opposite direction, back home. For us, the halfway mark was always just ahead, an elusive, sliding point that could only be reached by actually setting foot in the gymnasium.

At the end of one month, I announced to my astonished fellow travelers the results of some calculations I had carried out. At our present rate, we would cover a distance equal to that between Aachen and Vladivostok during the year. From then on, we charted our progress on a series of maps and soon passed the retreating German lines in Kiev on our relentless advance toward the Pacific Ocean.

Sometimes, however, we did arrive in Herzogenrath. This by no means assured us of a normal school day, for often the sirens would sound in the middle of a period. Then all classes lined up and marched, with a speed and discipline born of long experience, to the nearby shelter. There we assembled at preassigned places, and our teachers valiantly strove to resume where they had left off. But it was all in vain. The crowded conditions, noisy interference from other classes conducted in the same undivided space, and anxious listening for the explosion of bombs made concentration on our studies difficult, if not impossible. Under these circumstances, it was not surprising that I failed to learn anything during the academic year 1943/44.

CHAPTER 13

Since we no longer lived in Aachen, I had to switch my membership in the *Jungvolk* to Laurensberg. Service in my new troop was altogether different from what I had been used to before. No important functionary honored our rural squad with a visit to enlighten us on the three great themes of race, national history, and *Greater Germany's* role in the world, yet the *correct* answers to examination questions on these topics were an essential prerequisite for advancement in the youth organization. It seemed the Party had simply forgotten us, relegating us forever to the role of ordinary members of the lowest rank.

Nor did the local leadership make any serious effort to remedy the situation. Quite often, we were allowed to while away our time playing cards. Fortunately, I was beginning to have second thoughts on the desirability of being promoted to high office in the *Jungvolk* and thus gradually adjusted to the dearth of national-socialist ideas prevailing at Laurensberg.

To make up for our inadequate mental training, we went all out for physical fitness, running cross-country over hill and dale, pursuing rival *Jungvolk* squads through miles of woods along the German-Dutch frontier, picking up clues left at fixed intervals, finally closing in, pouncing on our victims, wrestling them to the ground, taking them prisoner, and shutting them up in our fortified POW camps. It was often dark when these war games were over, and at last, friend and foe, equally exhausted from the day's exertions, would gather around the campfire to plan the following week's maneuvers.

There was also a great deal of marching to the accompaniment of such patriotic songs as *"Heilig Vaterland"* (*Holy Fatherland*) and *"Denn wir fahren gegen Engeland"* (*For we go against England*) although the latter song struck me as absurdly inappropriate in view of the fact that we weren't going there at all. Rather it was the English who were going against us every day with their bombers.

My older cousin, Hans-Günter, was a *Jungzugführer* at Laurensberg. At first, I had been jealous of his rank and of the coveted black-and-green-braided cord he displayed on his breast as a symbol of his authority. Soon, however, he was drafted as a *Luftwaffenhelfer*. It had started with the seventh grade of our gymnasium, roughly equivalent to the third year in an American high school, but as the fortunes of war turned against Germany, the older soldiers, who up to then had manned the antiaircraft batteries at home, were desperately needed to shore up the crumbling front lines, and so the sixth and fifth graders, too, were sworn in to replace the departing men.

Hans-Günter at once discarded all *Hitler-Jugend* insignia, including the armband with the swastika which the *Luftwaffenhelfer* were supposed to wear on their blue air force coats. As he disdainfully told me, he and his friends wanted nothing to do with a youth organization that was meant for children, not for men.

On their next furlough, the fifteen- and sixteen-year-old boys put their new manhood to the test. Ostentatiously, in full uniform, they marched to a movie theater showing a film which was off limits to *juveniles under eighteen*. And the good-natured ticket taker actually let them in, reasoning perhaps that whoever is old enough to fight for his country is old enough to see an adult film. How we younger boys envied the others tasting of the unknown, forbidden fruit.

The *Luftwaffenhelfer* were to receive eighteen hours of regular academic instruction from their teachers who took daily trips out to the gun emplacements. This was considerably less than the thirty hours normally provided, but, as the Ministry of Science and Education pointed out with airtight logic, military training, plus the construction of entrenchments and earthworks, plus the demanding labor performed in firing the flak would easily compensate for the omission of physical education classes. Moreover, frills would be cut in favor of concentrating on core subjects. Lastly, the ministry optimistically announced, the challenge of the students' new responsibilities would enhance their maturity and seriousness of purpose to such an extent that they would accomplish at least as much, if not more than before, in the time available for schooling.

Hans-Günter was assigned to the flak battery on the golf course, a few kilometers from our house in Laurensberg. Of course, I went to see him as often as possible, far more impressed by his blue coat, visored cap, and belt buckle, all emblazoned with the air force eagle, than I had ever been by his black and green cord in the *Hitler-Jugend*.

He showed me his cannon and explained how it worked. There was a crew of six gunners for each heavy piece. The first two were responsible for the proper horizontal and vertical alignment of the gun. The third was in charge of loading it. This had to be done by an older soldier since the *Luftwaffenhelfer*, in spite of an extra ration of food granted them, were still too weak to put the forty-two-pound shells into a cannon barrel which pointed almost straight at the sky. The fourth, fifth, and sixth gunners hauled ammunition. Still other students operated radiolocation devices, range finders, searchlights, and communication equipment.

I was especially fascinated by the technical apparatus and soon felt confident I understood all procedures necessary to calculate the height and speed of a plane. My recent exertions in mathematics were finally paying off. If only the air force would allow me to put my knowledge to use, I would prove to them that I was fully as capable as these *Luftwaffenhelfer* who were only two grades ahead of me in school.

Hans-Günter and I also talked about our education. It seemed his was even spottier than mine. Often the battery was kept in a state of readiness throughout much of the night. Sometimes the guns would fire hundreds of rounds. Next morning, when the teacher arrived, all his students were sleeping in their barracks. Moreover, they found no interest in puzzling over a Latin text to discover why or when or how Caesar had won a certain battle two thousand years ago. There was not much time for assignments either, what with target practice, maintenance and cleaning of guns, building of earthworks, and other military duties.

This was the fifth year of the war. Everybody's clothes were shabby and worn. The poor schoolmasters who had to trek out to the batteries in all kinds of weather soon found their shoes falling apart. If they were lucky enough to own a bicycle, they felt the seats of their pants getting so threadbare that they no longer dared turn their backs to their students for fear of presenting a spectacle of indecent exposure. A cry for help went to Berlin where some high official in the Ministry of Armaments was moved to pity by the teachers' embarrassing plight. He had some new clothes distributed to each of them along with a stern warning to wear them only while on duty at the flak batteries or face charges of misappropriation of scarce war matériel.

During one of my visits at the golf course, I noticed some white rings painted around the barrel of Hans-Günter's cannon. He proudly explained that each of these represented one enemy plane shot down. With envious admiration, I watched the growing number of these marks. Here was my cousin *doing* something, active in the defense of his family and his city, while I was condemned to sitting idle in a basement, helplessly feeling the earth tremble around me.

My ambition for a career in the *Jungvolk* was gone, but I wished with all my heart I were just a little older so that I, too, could fire an antiaircraft gun. I would take revenge for the loss of my dear Liebi. She had been our *Kindermädchen* (nursemaid) for over ten years, and now she was dead, killed in a recent bombing raid. Yes, I longed to pay *them* back for this and to help protect all the people I loved and what was left of my city. I didn't change my mind when, shortly thereafter, the first *Luftwaffenhelfer* lost their lives in action.

CHAPTER 14

On Ash Wednesday, 1944, our family climbed to the Laurensberg parish church, which was perched on a hill to the north of our house. Even Father, in spite of his bad leg, walked up the steep path winding through fields and meadows.

In past years, the ritual for this holy day had meant rather little to me, but this time, I sensed its full significance as the pastor marked my forehead with a cross of ashes and spoke the words, "Dust thou art, and unto dust shalt thou return." Death was stalking the streets of Aachen. I had come to know it well. My life, too, could end any day.

A few weeks later, the Tuesday after Easter, we lived through one of the worst air raids of the war. The sirens had jolted us from our beds. Mother, her friend Frau Heser, Marita, and Hermann were already in the basement shelter, while Father and I stood in the garden, watching the beautiful, starry sky. Suddenly it was lit up clear as day by four *Christmas trees*. That's what we called the *Leuchtbomben* (flares) which showered the area to be bombed with cascades of light. Aachen would be the target of still another *Terrorangriff*.

We saw a plane being hit and hurtling to the ground as we hurried to the shelter. And then the explosions started. They seemed to be some distance away, yet the noise was fearful, an unremitting hailstorm of bursting bombs.

Frau Heser fell to her knees, wringing her hands, screaming, and praying throughout the attack. Nothing we did could stop her, and as if to make sure that God would hear her words above the din of the explosions, she raised her voice to its highest pitch. Of course, we were all frightened and praying within ourselves, but her genuflections and frenzied entreaties made us even more panicked. Soon Marita and Hermann were vying with her in strident supplications, and the walls of our little shelter reverberated with their joined prayers.

When it was all over, we went outside, still shaking. A solid wall of fire and smoke rose against the sky in the distance over my beloved city.

I remember walking through the streets two days later. There was no transportation, no water, and no electricity. Digging crews were still at work clearing the rubble and looking for survivors or corpses. Over one thousand five hundred people had been killed, and another one thousand injured. The area around the main railroad station and the residential and spa district of Burtscheid were one vast expanse of ruins.

Observing this scene of desolation, I shook as much as I had during the air raid. I was sick at heart when I returned home yet thankful to be still alive. Though many bombs had fallen on the woods to the south of Aachen, I persisted in my belief that rural Laurensberg was secure. After all, no damage had occurred anywhere near our house. Moreover, my aunt and uncle, who had long since left for an even safer place, a forester's lodge close to the border with Luxemburg, had constructed a concrete shelter into the basement of their villa. True, its walls were only about ten inches thick, but it did have a heavy steel door and an emergency exit into the driveway. I knew it could not withstand a direct hit. Still, it would easily protect us from any unlikely explosion nearby or from the weight of the collapsing house.

The next major air raid came on May 25, 1944. Never before and never since had death been so close to me, just a few yards away. The whistling sound of the bombs made us realize instinctively that they were headed straight for us. Amid earsplitting explosions, the whole house jumped on its foundations. Frightened to death, pale as ashes, we crouched in our shelter. Father and Mother enclosed us in their arms, shielding us with their bodies.

We got out through the emergency exit. The villa had been blown to pieces. The rubble was in flames. Dozens of bombs had literally plowed up the surrounding field. Later, in the summer, we would go bathing there. Three adjoining craters made a perfect swimming pool teeming with frogs. But now, we set out for our friends' house, the Fussgänger's place, where I had done my forbidden skiing more than two years ago.

Our parents led the way. "Thank God for sparing us this time," said Mother, "if only this cursed war were over. If only we get through it alive and unmaimed."

Father and Mother moved slowly and bent over, with tired steps. Leaning on his cane, he limped along his free hand around her waist. As I watched them walking into the night, I knew that we could keep going as long as we had our parents. Beyond all losses and beyond all suffering, there would be a new beginning, even beyond this war. Father and Mother gave me the strength to believe in this.

We arrived at the Fussgänger's empty-handed—with nothing but the clothes on our back.

CHAPTER 15

Fortunately, our friends' spacious house had escaped damage, and Frau Fussgänger generously invited us to stay with them. Our faces still bore the mark of the night's terror, yet I could feel a sense of relief, almost of joy, in each of us as we sat around the dining room table sipping ersatz coffee and warm milk. Nobody wanted to talk about the air raid. We had survived it and knew that in all probability there would not be another big one for some time, perhaps a few weeks or, if we were lucky, a few months. And by then the war might be nearly over. This thought suddenly flashed through my mind, and with it, the realization that our odds of coming through the ordeal alive improved with each passing day.

In the morning, our friends searched their scant wardrobes for anything they could spare and soon handed us a badly needed, if ill-fitting, assortment of clothes. My lanky figure looked ludicrous in a pair of pants twice as wide and half as long as my anatomy required, but this outfit would have to do until the local office could process our application for hardship coupons to which we were entitled after having lost all our possessions.

Herr Fussgänger owned the dye works in Laurensberg. His little factory was humming full speed to turn out cloth for *Wehrmacht* uniforms. I was fascinated by the vats of steaming acid dyestuff and the clanking jiggers and presses. There were few Germans among the workers now. They had been drafted into the army or shifted to essential war industries. To replace them, the government had sent Herr Fussgänger a group of Ukrainian women.

I listened to the sound of their conversation amid the din of the machines, not understanding a word of what they were saying. One of them was singing a lilting, melancholy song as she guided a strip of fabric along an overhead metal runner. Suddenly, she spied the intent face of a curious boy in baggy, too-short pants and burst out laughing. Soon, all the women noticed the cause of her merriment. They looked at me and smiled. And I smiled back.

This was the first time I had met any of these *Untermenschen* (subhumans) as the Nazi propaganda called the Slavs deported from Eastern Europe. A while ago, Father had received a circular letter, marked *secret*, from the education section of our *Gau* (district). It had gone to all party members and contained the *Ten Commandments* concerning the correct treatment of Slavs and other inferior peoples. There was an immutable dividing line, drawn in blood, between them and us. Every National Socialist had a sacred duty to live and preach this truth to his fellow Germans. The letter concluded by reminding its readers of the Führer's saying, "The only immortality in the world lies in the preservation of national purity."

Faithful to the Party's order, Father had begun his educational mission at once. One evening after dinner, he gave us his commentary on the new rules of conduct as set forth in the secret missive, leaving no doubt in our minds that he considered *these* ten commandments anything but divinely-inspired. When he finished his sarcastic remarks, Mother read a brief passage from the Gospel: "For I was hungry, and ye gave me food; I was thirsty, and ye gave me drink; I was a stranger, and ye took me in; naked, and ye clothed me; I was sick, and ye visited me; in prison, and ye came unto me... Verily, I say unto you, Inasmuch as ye did it unto one of the least of these my brethren, ye did it unto me."

Though my parents' words had cleared away much of the fog left in my mind by the endless propaganda enclosing us, I found it difficult to forget entirely all the stories I had heard. Weren't those people from the East a vulgar herd, untutored, loutish yokels at best, brutal vandals at worst? That's what I had been taught. and part of this teaching continued to haunt some dark recesses of my subconscious against my better knowledge. It was rather like my feelings toward *Sankt Nikolaus* who always visited our home on the sixth day of December in the company of his servant *Knecht Ruprecht*. The latter carried a rod to chastise disobedient children and a bag into which he threatened to throw the most recalcitrant wrongdoers. *Sankt Nikolaus* seemed to know all my sins, and *Ruprecht* made ominous moves in my direction. But the good saint would finally restrain him and, finding some redeeming virtue in my flawed character, would forgive me once more and hand me a present.

Even after an older friend had convinced me that *Sankt Nikolaus* and *Knecht Ruprecht* were just ordinary humans in disguise, I still had shaken with fear this past December. It was hard to shed a childhood belief overnight.

Thus, it was with the Russian prisoners of war I had seen at the golf course. They were called *Hiwis*, short for *Hilfswillige* (willing to help), and had been lured by promises of better treatment and more food to trade the rigors of POW camp for service with the flak batteries. To be sure, those Russians didn't look at all *subhuman*, peeling potatoes or polishing guns. Hans-Günter told me that they hauled shells during air raids. One of them had even helped him with a math problem one day. Still, one can never be certain. It might be safer to keep one's distance from them just in case they were really as bad as I had been taught to believe.

But the Ukrainians in the dye works managed, within a few minutes, to destroy once and for all any lingering thought that Slavs might be *Untermenschen*. The slender, beautiful, kerchiefed young woman who had interrupted her song to laugh at my ill-fitting pants spoke a little German. She was from Nikolayev on the Bug River, near the Black Sea. I looked it up in an atlas and found it well to the east of the current German lines. So her town had already been retaken by Soviet forces. Katja confirmed this. She was well-informed about the course of the war and radiated a quiet, unshakable faith in her country's eventual triumph.

Later she showed me a faded, crumpled picture of her husband, a lieutenant in the Soviet army. She also taught me one verse of the haunting song she had been singing when I had first seen her. Katja was infinitely patient in helping me pronounce the strange words correctly. At last, I had mastered this difficult task to her satisfaction. Upon a sign from her, all the women started singing, and I chimed in. Up to then, the supervisor of Katja's workshop had pretended not to notice any of my dealings with her charges, which surely violated the ten commandments, but this joint singing went too far for her. She quickly left the room so as not to witness this altogether forbidden intercourse between an Aryan boy and a group of Ukrainian women.

Twice during our stay with the Fussgängers, I was able to save a piece of bread from my evening meal and to slip it to Katja the next morning. The day we had to leave was a sad one for me and, I think, for Katja too. We had grown fond of each other.

CHAPTER 16

We moved into a villa on the side of the Lousberg. Below the house stretched a lovely, terraced garden, full of flowers, and beyond, in the hollow, lay the heart of the city, a panoramic expanse of ruins instead of the beautiful Aachen we had known a few years ago. Across the street rose the Lousberg, a wooded hill which retained some of its parklike character in spite of many uprooted trees and bomb craters. These were a reminder, if we needed one, that a location on the outskirts of the city offered little assurance of escape from aerial bombardment.

Luckily there was a public air raid shelter a five-minute run from the house. So at least we did not have to depend on a shaky basement for protection. If there was a really bad attack, we could hope to scurry in good time to the safety of the bombproof concrete shelter.

The villa was quite well equipped with dishes, cutlery, linen, and other essentials. We had received permission from the owners, who had long ago fled to southern Germany, to use their house and its belongings until their return. Before they could think of coming back, however, other events intervened.

In June 1944, Allied troops landed in Normandy. I had spent countless hours in school, during art class, drawing the *Atlantic Wall*, a supposedly impenetrable series of defense works guarding the Atlantic coastline of France. My teacher, though not overly impressed with the artistic quality of my output, wholeheartedly approved my choice of subject matter. Thus, I continued, with his encouragement, to invent ever new variations on the single theme of bulwarks and bastions. Unburdened by any firsthand acquaintance with these fortifications, I let my imagination run wild, disdainful of taking my inspiration from the homely *Westwall* with its familiar bunkers and dragons' teeth, which crisscrossed the landscape all around Aachen.

A month after the Allied landings, the *Atlantic Wall* turned out to have been far more formidable on paper—in my sketchbook—than on the French coast. Foreign armies were now advancing from the west as well as the east. It was just a question of time before Germany herself would become the battleground. The Thousand Year Reich was doomed.

Behind the last battle of this war stands our victory. This slogan, painted in big letters on the wall of a nearby playground, all at once seemed empty to me. Or rather, it acquired a new meaning. Beyond the last battle, there might be *peace.* It would be a victory of sorts to survive till then.

After the abortive attempt on Hitler's life in July 1944, a good many party orators, showing themselves well versed in biblical scholarship, bandied about chapter and verse to prove that the Lord had held his helping hand over our Führer. I found this sudden display of piety surprising. It was hard to believe that the Psalmist had been thinking of Adolf Hitler when he wrote the words: "Thou shalt not be afraid for the terror by night, nor for the arrow that flieth by day, nor for the pestilence that walketh in darkness, nor for the destruction that wasteth at noonday. A thousand shall fall at thy side, and ten thousand at thy right hand, but it shall not come nigh thee."

Though Stauffenberg's bomb failed to undo Hitler, it did tear away the nimbus of power and authority from my image of the Führer. A god—or at least a godling—had escaped by the skin of his teeth. He had been knocked off his pedestal, and his feet turned out to be of clay. For the first time, I was able to imagine a future without him.

As the front moved closer, the order went out for all citizens to evacuate Aachen, which was declared a fortress to be defended at all costs. So once again, we packed our belongings, few by then, and in late August took one of the last trains to leave the city.

CHAPTER 17

When the train arrived at the station Aachen West, it was already packed full. Passenger cars, box cars, and stock cars, even the caboose, were overloaded with refugees. Only the flatcar at the rear with its swivel-mounted antiaircraft gun had room to spare, but the crew refused to take any civilians aboard. And so a wild scuffling and scrambling began. One old man pulled himself in through a window, dragging his limp wife after him. Others climbed onto the roofs of the railway carriages. We managed to elbow our way through the door of a passenger car. The open WC was occupied by four cramped adults. One child stood on top of the toilet bowl. Shoulder to shoulder with our jostling neighbors, the five of us formed a tight, penned up group near the end of the corridor.

The journey was uneventful until we passed Herzogenrath. We had heard a distant siren sound the full alarm signal sometime ago. Suddenly, low-flying planes appeared on the horizon. We could not see them from our place in the train, but our excited fellow travelers by the window kept us informed, "Mosquitoes. Six of them. Heading east."

These were fighters and light bombers of the Royal Air Force. The words announcing them were cut off by explosions ripping through the air. Our train chugged along amid the roar of antiaircraft fire and the bursting of bombs. "I think they are attacking the coal mines," I heard someone say. Then an earsplitting blast made the train jump on its tracks. Had it been hit or derailed? No, but we began to slow down and came to a halt.

Passengers leaped through the windows, fought their way through the doors, and threw themselves down in the field by the tracks. The rushing crowd sucked us along. I remember giving a hand to Father as he was pushed out of the train. He landed on his bad leg and collapsed but was able to crawl a few yards, grimacing with pain. Mother, Marita, and Hermann already lay low in a plot of cabbages.

The *flak* on our flatcar was firing nonstop. Soon it became clear, however, that we were not the target of the air raid. A single errant bomb had missed us by a hair's breadth. All the others fell farther east.

We brushed the dirt off our clothes and got back on the train. As if by magic, everybody reoccupied the same place as before—the same four adults in the WC and the same child on the toilet bowl. We were all too spent to fight each other.

After a bombing raid, I always felt an uncontrollable rage. Why did they have to hunt us day and night, even as we were fleeing from our hometown? I rejoiced when I saw an enemy plane shot down and longed for the day I would be a *Luftwaffenhelfer*. In the meantime, I took comfort in the *Vergeltungswaffen* (retaliatory weapons), the V I and later, the V II rockets, striking at London.

The train stopped. We had arrived in Kempen, about fifteen miles west of the Rhine River, even closer to the Dutch frontier. The war would, of course, catch up with us here before long, but we could reasonably expect a country town to be defended less fiercely than the city of Aachen.

We walked a short distance from the railroad station. Except for a few ruins, Kempen seemed untouched by war. The Burgring Avenue skirted the spacious park surrounding the fortress-like castle or *Burg* with its two round brick towers. Up ahead, we saw Uncle Anton and Aunt Anna's three-story house, the oriel on the second floor, the veranda below, and the double-winged iron gate to the garden, and there, perched in a plum tree, Uncle Anton in his inevitable white shorts and loose-fitting linen jacket, was picking the season's last plums. When he caught sight of us, he climbed down with a nimbleness belying his age—he had been retired from his job as director of a chemical company for several years—and greeted us with a hearty, "Welcome. I can use some help with my gardening." Aunt Anna embraced each of us. We had found a haven with them.

A flock of chickens roamed in the orchard under trees still loaded with apples and pears, peaches, and plums. Beyond the fence stretched neat long rows of vegetables. Along the wall ran the raspberry, gooseberry, and currant bushes.

"There will be enough to eat here," I told myself, as I surveyed this Garden of Eden. Aunt Anna must have read our thoughts, for she handed us ripe peaches. "Here, eat these while I fix dinner. How would you like dumplings with plums?" She knew well this was a favorite dish with us children.

CHAPTER 18

The first floor of the house in Kempen consisted of a living room, a formal and an everyday dining room, the kitchen, a drawing room, and the veranda. Upstairs were five bedrooms. So there was ample space for our family as well as for other relatives who took temporary refuge there.

My uncle and aunt's four sons had all gone off to war. Two were already dead. Only the eldest was to survive. I remember his homecoming well. For weeks, Aunt Anna had been sleeping very little, watching and waiting for his return. Uncle Anton could not persuade her that there was no good reason to expect him. She insisted she *knew* he was on his way home. When she heard the gentle tapping at the door in the darkness of night, she was up at once, rushed down, and held her one remaining son with all the love she had borne the four of them. He had defied the ten o'clock curfew imposed on the German population and made his way through alleyways and private gardens to the backdoor.

But this reunion was not to be until July 1945, after the war. We were still in the fall of 1944. My parents enrolled me at the municipal gymnasium. Education, however, proved as evanescent as in the endless streetcar journeys to and from Herzogenrath. School was usually canceled. We boys were handed shovel or pickaxe and marched out the highway to Wachtendonk. There we would spend the day digging trenches and foxholes on both sides of the road. These fortifications, a local party leader explained, were our contribution to the *Endsieg* (final victory).

Twice American planes fired their guns at us. My fellow students, not yet accustomed to such events, shook with fear as they crouched in the half-finished ditches, while I, with childish bravado, displayed the sangfroid of one inured to air raids. Later, we discovered some empty shells and took them home to scare our parents and boast of our narrow escape.

Sometimes, a few bombs dropped on Kempen. It was useless to replace the shattered windowpanes, for glass was hard to come by. And even if you were lucky enough to find some, it would last only a brief time before it was blown out again. Moreover, it was dangerous. One day, Mother was taking a nap after lunch when pieces of glass came flying all over her bed. She was bleeding profusely. From then on, we simply nailed cardboard or plywood over the window frames.

Father had always loved to tease us or tell a tall story. As a boy, he had been caught in a deluge on his way to school and surprised his teacher by swimming into the classroom through the window, his pencil box floating before him. Another time, a lion had chased Mother and him up a tree. He had fought off the monster with his cane and finally succeeded in ramming the whole length of the stick down his gaping gullet. Stiffened by the indigestible object within him, the king of beasts had helplessly watched my parents make their getaway.

In Kempen, Father did not tell stories anymore. He looked careworn, harrowed, and deadly serious. To be sure, the crow's feet were still at the corners of his eyes, but they were all that was left of his love of laughter. Later, I understood how much this enforced idleness, the uncertainty of life, and the knowledge that in his late fifties he would have to return to a pile of rubble and start all over again, must have weighed on him.

Uncle Anton was a fanatical gardener. He would tolerate not a single weed among his flowers and vegetables. Every tree had to be pruned just right, the compost heap tended with loving care, the harvest gathered and recorded in the big black ledger. In a wheelbarrow, my brother and I got manure from a farmer and dug it into the soil. There was plenty of work for us. Uncle Anton did not even let up after Hermann innocently pulled out an entire row of carrots in the belief that they were unwanted grass. Still, I found time to roller-skate on the smooth asphalt road past our trenches to Wachtendonk and to fall in love.

Once when Leonore was chatting with my sister, who was excused from gardening but helped instead with canning, pickling, and preserving, I had to feign a sprained ankle to win some respite from the ever-pressing horticultural tasks. I limped convincingly to the veranda, chased away Marita, and had Leonore all to myself. Sitting close to her, I smugly watched a doubting Hermann and an equally skeptical Uncle Anton build a root cellar.

Soon, classes at the gymnasium stopped altogether. Far from rejoicing in this indefinite vacation, I felt actually deprived, for school had been interrupted so often that my mind was famished for knowledge. I began to read voraciously on my own. It was then that Uncle Anton stepped forward and took charge of my education. Every morning after returning from Holy Mass, he summoned me to the drawing room to instruct me in the various subjects, competently in Latin, mathematics, and science, rather poorly in English, of which he remembered little more than I had already learned. But the most unforgettable lessons were his free roaming questions about history, literature, and philosophy, ending invariably with a demonstration of the incompatibility of Christian values and the Nazi ideology.

Once, a neighbor came to visit and held forth on the need to stand by the Führer who surely, in this desperate hour, would yet find a way of crushing the enemies of his Reich. Perhaps he was trying to trap my parents, uncle, or aunt into making an imprudent, disloyal reply. Before that could happen, I quickly quoted one of Uncle Anton's favorite Latin sayings: *"Si tacuisses, philosophus mansisses,"* ("If you had kept quiet, you would have remained a philosopher.") Upon the Party official's suspicious insistence, I translated this as "It is the philosopher's calling to tell the truth." He left satisfied, no doubt thinking of himself as a truthful sage.

Uncle Anton pulled one of the volumes from his bookcase, inscribed it ceremoniously with the words *To my godson Herbert Anton* and handed it to me as a present. From then on, whenever he was especially pleased with my progress, he rewarded me with a book, published, of course, prior to 1933 and thus uninfected by the *cancer of National Socialism* as he put it. I still own several of these today, including his copy of *De Imitatione Christi* by Thomas a Kempis, who was born in this small town where we had found shelter in the closing months of the war.

We were all anxiously waiting for news about the fate of our city. "Aachen is defended by elite troops on whom our enemies will break their teeth," Propaganda Minister Goebbels had boasted in one of his morale-building proclamations to a doubting nation. "Charlemagne's capital will become a Stalingrad for the invaders."

Naturally, we wanted to know what was really happening. So in the evening, before going to bed, we often sat in the living room with the curtains drawn and the door shut tight. One of us children stood guard outside, behind a bush, to give a warning signal if our neighbor or any stranger were approaching. The rest of us would listen to the BBC. On October 21, 1944, it announced that American forces had captured Aachen after bitter house-to-house fighting. A few days later, a German broadcast admitted the fall of the city to foreign invaders. No mention was made of Goebbels's empty promises, which had been trumpeted about so noisily only a short while ago.

The end was near. We determined to flee no further. Come what may, we would wait out the war in Kempen.

CHAPTER 19

We waited longer than we had expected. A harsh winter and the last German counteroffensive temporarily stalled the Allied advance. This breathing space gave party functionaries the time to carry out Hitler's decree establishing the *Volkssturm* (people's storm), whose local unit was placed under the command of Dr. Pohl, a dentist. No doubt his experience as a captain in World War I and his enduring ability—attested to by all his patients—to hold the drill with a firm hand in spite of his venerable age qualified him well for this position of leadership. And so he marched his troops, consisting of men over fifty and boys who had not yet been called into service as *Luftwaffenhelfer*, through the streets of Kempen to the training grounds where they learned how to wield a rifle, bazooka, or hand grenade.

Father had been declared unfit for active duty because of the injury suffered in 1914. Uncle Anton was too old even for the *Volkssturm*. And I was too young.

> Jugend und Alter—Mann für Mann
> umklammem das Hakenkreuzbanner.
> Ob Bürger, ob Bauer, ob Arbeitsmann,
> sie schwingen das Schwert und den Hammer
> für Hitler, für Freiheit, für Arbeit, für Brot.
> Deutschland erwache, ende die Not!
> Volk ans Gewehr! Volk ans Gewehr!

Young and old—man for man
clasp the swastika banner.
Citizen, farmer and laboring man,
they all swing the sword and the hammer
for Hitler, for freedom, for work and for bread.
Germany awaken, end your distress!
Nation to arms! To arms!

I heard this song often in the winter of 1944/45 as the *Volkssturm* prepared for the defense of Kempen, while I stood on the sidelines, a passive observer lost in daydreams. Scenes from the past sprang up before my eyes in a series of vivid flashbacks: the head of my school calling a special assembly to honor a former student, on leave from the war. I was hanging on the young officer's lips so as not to miss a word of his glorious exploits, staring with envious admiration at the *Ritterkreuz* (Knight's Cross) around the hero's neck and not only I, my fellow students, our teachers, the director himself, all being struck with awe.

I saw myself again at the battery, listening to Hans-Günter explain with manly pride the significance of the white rings on the barrel of his cannon. Once more the *Gauleiter* (regional party leader) raised his strident voice against the Allies' demand for unconditional surrender. I shuddered as he described what was in store for us. "You will be like slaves, driven from your homes, your women dishonored, your country dismembered unless you rise up as one man to smite the enemy." I remembered a newspaper picture, a group of boys, some as young as thirteen, being decorated with the Iron Cross for bravery in knocking out Russian tanks.

"*Volk ans Gewehr! Volk ans Gewehr!*" The words of the *Volkssturm* marching by roused me from my trance. Yes, to be a soldier was to be a man, to be taken seriously, and to make the great leap across the gulf between childhood and manhood.

I was almost thirteen, ready to be a man myself. For the Führer, I was no longer willing to *swing the sword and the hammer*, nor for his party, but for freedom and work and bread, for the defense of my country and family, I would give my all.

Dimly aware that there was something wrong with my resolve, I dared no more than hint at it at home. Father laughed just as I had feared. He would not take me seriously, but neither would he let me off the hook. Did I really think the motley, untrained, ill-equipped *Volkssturm* was going to turn the tide of the war even if its crew of old men and children were able to entrench themselves in the ditches I had dug? Did I not see that every day thousands were being killed? More of our cities destroyed? Misery heaped upon misery? That the best thing for our country was a quick end to the fighting and to Hitler's rule?

In my heart and mind, I agreed with everything he said. Yet somewhere within me still echoed the slogans that had been hammered into us at the *Jungvolk* meetings. Fortitude. Manliness. Duty. Sacrifice. Heroism. Laying down one's life for a noble cause. But where *was* the noble cause?

Mother answered me, "There is none. We are passing through the zero hour of history when there is no longer any past and not yet a future. But to forge a new life, for yourself and your country, out of the chaos of this moment, you will need all the strength, courage, and spirit of sacrifice you can muster. Do not waste these qualities. They are rare and precious like pearls. Do not cast them before swine lest they trample them under their feet."

I had no doubt whom she meant by *swine*. All at once, I felt a surge of love for my parents. Rushing up to them, I embraced them with such impulsive fervor that they were startled into stillness. Once again, a talk with them had helped clear the mists of my confusion and silenced the voice of the serpent. Where would I be without Father and Mother? Throughout my insecure childhood, they had guided me safely on a long night's journey into day. Even now they had taken me seriously after all, reasoning with me as if I were a man. They were wrong, of course. I had only been a child trying to play man and had let a pubescent lust for adventure seduce me into wanting to join the *Volkssturm*.

As the front lines moved closer, we could hear the constant rumble of artillery fire. Many families spent a good part of the day and night in the castle's massive basement, which offered protection

from the shelling and bombing. In early March 1945, a first lieutenant arrived in Kempen with forty regular army men to shore up
the town's defenses. He set up his command post in the little concrete
shelter, which had been built on top of one of the round brick towers, searching the horizon with his high-powered binoculars for any
sign of the approaching enemy. I was often with him up there when
there was a lull in the din of battle.

For lack of any other able-bodied men, the lieutenant appointed
me *Melder* (dispatch runner). I was, he explained, to take his messages to the front, informing his soldiers and the *Volkssturm* of his
tactical decisions. At last, I had a role, however unofficial, to play in
the war, but the call to the colors came too late to give me any joy. I
was already looking beyond Armageddon toward the future.

As it turned out, I had little to do. The lieutenant spotted a con-
tingent of about a hundred Americans supported by some tanks in
the distance. "That's too much," he declared matter-of-factly, "I am
going to get out with my men. You can tell the *Volkssturm* I bid them
Godspeed. They are on their own. Good luck to you." He patted me
on the head and disappeared. Five minutes later, I saw his car and
two trucks loaded with soldiers head east toward the Rhine.

I thought it my duty to deliver my one and only message as a
dispatch runner. Dr. Pohl ought to know that the *Volkssturm* was
alone in the battle for Kempen. As I left the castle for his defensive
position, I saw the dentist, leaning on one of his men, limp across the
park. He was dragging his left leg, his face distorted with pain. "I've
been hit," he groaned, "help me."

Together we moved him, with infinite care, to the steel door
facing the sunken ground of the grassy moat. My heart went out to
Dr. Pohl, who was in such visible agony, worse than any he had ever
inflicted on his patients with the drill. What ill fortune for him to
suffer a crippling injury on his first and last day of combat in this
long war. If only he would not lose his leg.

We knocked on the door. Slowly it opened a crack. Frau
Grooten popped out her head. She seemed surprised that we were
not the vanguard of the Americans and quickly withdrew the bottle
of *Schnapps* she held out to us.

The dentist slid down, gripping his painful leg. Someone brought a stretcher. We carried the wounded man to the back room. A doctor and a nurse rushed in to give first aid. They cut open the trousers and found nothing. No matter which way they turned the *Volkssturm* commander, they could not discover the slightest scratch on him.

Dr. Pohl insisted his leg was *hors de combat.* Something had to be seriously wrong with him. He supposed it was internal injury, but neither the physician nor the nurse was able to confirm the dentist's diagnosis.

The man who had helped him back to the castle started laughing out loud, less *at* his commander, however, than *with* relief. There was going to be no battle. How could there be with the leader of the *Volkssturm* on the operating table? He ran off to tell the good news to the rest of the group.

Aunt Anna suggested hoisting a white flag. I dashed to our house, got a bed sheet, and suspended it from the battlements of the castle tower.

Soon, Dr. Pohl regained the use of his leg. Word of the miraculous healing spread throughout the large basement and produced much mirth and snickering, but Uncle Anton remarked dryly that the dentist deserved a medal for his common sense. "Now Kempen will perhaps fall without the loss of a single life."

He was right. Within an hour, the steel door shook under the pounding of rifle butts. Frau Grooten opened and greeted the GIs outside with the only English she knew, "Goot tay. I huff *Schnapps* for you." They pushed her aside and swarmed into the basement, knocking down doors and breaking into closets. In one of them, two revolvers were discovered. Suspicious now, the soldiers pointed their guns at us. Several people at once tried to explain we had known nothing about this cache of arms, and since, in fact, no more weapons were found, the GIs soon turned friendly. They uncorked Frau Grooten's precious *Schnapps* and guzzled it down to the last drop, exclaiming, *"Gut, gut"* after every gulp.

The *battle* for Kempen was over. Not a shot had been fired in its defense. Mother's zero hour was ringing in the end of the Third Reich and the start of an unknowable future.

CHAPTER 20

Shortly after we had gone back home, four GIs banged on our door. They had come to search the house. "Do you have any weapons?"

"No."

"Any cameras?" My absurdly honest uncle produced his *Voigtländer* and then looked inquiringly at my parents who stood their ground and said nothing. "Where is your *Leica*?" asked Uncle Anton. sternly. Upon hearing the word *Leica*, the soldiers pricked up their ears and, brandishing their guns, demanded to see it.

Mother had no choice but to get it from its hiding place behind the canned tomatoes, on a shelf in the basement.

"All cameras are confiscated for reasons of military security," declared the Americans. They were about to leave when Mother resolutely barred their way. She had known hunger at the end of the World War I and was determined to keep her family from starving. The *Leica* was one of our few remaining possessions. It would be a valuable object in trade, which could help us survive in the hard times to come.

"I want a receipt for the camera," Mother insisted in halting, mispronounced English left over from her schoolgirl days. The startled GIs seemed at a loss for words. At last, one of them tore a sheet from a notepad and obligingly wrote *One Voigtländer, one Leica confiscated* on it. Underneath, he scribbled our names, the date, and an illegible signature. Needless to say, we never saw our cameras again. The receipt proved to be utterly worthless, but we all admired Mother's courage in her first encounter with the occupation authorities.

A few hours later, all males aged eighteen and over were rounded up and herded into the basement of the *Katasteramt* (Tax and Land Registry Office). By curfew time, Father and Uncle Anton had not returned. We spent an anxious night worrying about their fate. Recently, the Ministry of National Enlightenment and Propaganda had circulated accounts of heinous atrocities committed in East Prussia. Hundreds of civilians had been forced to lie down to be crushed by advancing Russian tanks, we had been told. What would happen to Father and Uncle Anton? To the men of Kempen?

Next morning, we learned with relief that they were still in their prison. Rumors started flying: they would be deported. They were being held as hostages. They would be shot if there were any signs of resistance or sabotage.

The forlorn women organized a children's crusade to save the men. Along with scores of other boys and girls, Marita, Hermann, and I marched to the *Katasteramt*, laid siege to it, and pleaded with the guards to give our fathers back to us. The American soldiers tried to persuade us to go home. The men would be released in the afternoon. When our wailing and weeping did not cease, they allowed some of their prisoners to come up into the courtyard to assure us they were all right. Uncle Anton was among these. It wasn't comfortable spending the night on a wooden bench in the basement, he said, but they were all safe and sound and had been promised they would be released later in the day.

These words comforted us, but we still would not quit the field. We were determined to wait until curfew time and beyond, if necessary, to prevent our fathers from being spirited away.

The Americans kept their word. In the afternoon, they let their captives go, one by one, after taking down their names, personal data, and Nazi affiliations. Nobody was to leave Kempen without a permit, upon threat of severe punishment.

Every few minutes, the door of the *Katasteramt* swung open. Women and children rushed forward to claim their husbands and fathers. At last, Father appeared on the steps. We hugged him as tightly as if he had been gone for months. Then it was Uncle Anton's turn. Triumphantly we escorted them back home, encouraged by this latest experience with our new rulers.

CHAPTER 21

Food was getting extremely scarce. The meager German supplies were no longer coming in, and the occupation forces had not yet set up a system of providing for the civilian population. I knew that roving bands of people were breaking into stores whose owners had fled from Kempen at the last moment and proposed to go foraging myself.

Uncle Anton wanted none of this *looting*. To steal was a sin, and *the wages of sin is death*. He did not foresee that pilfering would soon receive the blessing of the church. In the winter of 1945/46, freezing Germans robbed the trains which were carrying cargos of coal abroad as war reparations. It was then that Cardinal Frings of Cologne put his authority squarely behind such thefts provided a person took no more than was necessary to sustain life and had no other means of obtaining the goods. And so a new verb enriched our language. We went *fringsing* in good conscience. But in the spring of 1945, this doctrine had not yet been promulgated, and Uncle Anton stuck to safer, more traditional morals.

The rest of us, less concerned with moral philosophy than immediate needs, held a family council behind Uncle Anton's back. Unanimously, we accepted Mother's suggestion that we should keep an exact record of what I might take and pay the owner later. Of course, money was next to worthless. What really mattered were ration coupons, but Mother's idea seemed an ingenious way of reconciling the demands of honesty with those of our stomachs.

I set out on my search for food. Between our house and the railroad station was a grocery store, its window boarded over, the door securely bolted. My pounding and shouting produced no sign of the proprietor. It did, however, attract a crowd of would-be burglars. Improvising a battering ram from the charred beam of a nearby bombed-out building, we broke through the entrance. I was filled with a mixture of guilt, pride, and fear as I ladled flour, noodles, sugar, dried beans, and powdered milk into my paper bags and seized the special prize of a can of lard. Once safely outside, I breathed a prayer of thanks for my spoils. Surely, the gifts I bore were as precious as the gold, myrrh, and frankincense the three wise men had offered the newborn child in Bethlehem. Head high and arms full, I made my way home.

Good tidings awaited me there. The Americans who had occupied the *Lebkuchenfabrik* (gingerbread factory) on the outskirts of town were giving away all the supplies left in the warehouse, one loaf to a person. Mother, Marita, and Hermann were already standing in line, and I rushed off to receive my share of the manna dispensed by the powers on high. Just before curfew time, I was rewarded with a *Lebkuchen*. The spicy aroma made me forget my aching feet.

Our potatoes and canned garden produce, supplemented by the day's haul from the grocery store and the gift of gingerbread, enabled us to get by until an orderly food distribution system was established. Before new ration coupons were issued, however, inspectors visited every house. Their job was to fix a quota of meat and eggs to be delivered to the authorities by any family lucky enough to own such animals as chickens, pigs, or rabbits. Uncle Anton took the officials to his chicken coop, but the birds, frightened by the intruders, fluttered about so wildly that the men had no end of trouble counting them. At last, they announced the result of their census: eight hens and one rooster. These numbers were duly entered into a register, which Uncle Anton was asked to sign.

Indignantly, he pushed aside the black book, insisting he was the owner of ten chickens and one cock. Yet much to his consternation, his own meticulous recount succeeded only in confirming the previous total of nine.

I wondered out loud what could have caused the excited crowing and clucking I had heard the night before. Maybe thieves had broken into the coop and made off with our two hens?

The inspectors agreed this was a plausible explanation for the mystery of the missing chickens and, after advising my angry uncle to padlock and barricade his animals securely henceforth, obtained his signature to the number nine.

Within minutes of the officials' departure, the flock grew to eleven again as Mother and Aunt Anna rescued two halfchoked chickens from underneath a pile of clothes in the big oak wardrobe. I had seen them seize the fowls by their necks and carry them through the backdoor of the house just as Uncle Anton led the census takers down the veranda steps. Now I congratulated Mother on her quick action. "If the city fathers of Aachen ever decide to replace the melted-down statute of the *Hühnerdieb* (chicken thief)," I said, "they ought to redesign the monument so as to show you stuffing your bird into a wardrobe." She kissed me with a happy smile, delighted by my fanciful suggestion.

Shortly thereafter, our house was requisitioned as quarters for several officers. We had to leave. All our pleading was in vain. Neither my uncle and aunt's advanced age nor the size of our family group could persuade the occupation authorities to set aside their order. They did allow us, however, to tend the garden and look after our priceless chickens.

We found an empty villa near the gymnasium. I climbed through a shattered window and let the others in. While the adults examined the premises, we children began to stake out claims to our favorite rooms. Everything was in pretty good shape, and we decided to move in. All day long, Hermann and I pushed and pulled our handcart through the streets of Kempen, transporting the belongings we were permitted to take to our new home.

A few days later, I ferried a cartload of dirty clothes and sheets to the house from which we had been expelled. Aunt Anna and Marita were going to do the laundry in the washhouse between the yard and the little orchard. As we entered through the garden gate, Aunt Anna suddenly stopped and stared ahead, her eyes bulging with disbelief. There, sprawled on the lawn, among the rose bushes, stood her leather armchairs and couch, the oak table, and three of the dining room chairs. They had been left out in the rain overnight. Puddles of water still filled the hollows of the seats.

This sight was too much for Aunt Anna to bear. Throwing all caution to the winds, she stalked into the house and proceeded to castigate its new tenants with a tirade of *fortissimo* reproaches. After what seemed to us an endless wait, her black figure—she wore nothing but black since the death of her sons—at last emerged on the veranda. Four young officers slunk behind her, their faces as red with shame as hers was blotched with indignation. Aunt Anna continued to pour forth a stream of reprimands, gesticulating wildly and beating her hands on the couch, so that the water splashed all over her gown.

The Americans looked like guilty schoolboys accepting a well-deserved scolding from their teacher. There was no need for an interpreter. Aunt Anna's meaning was crystal clear. When her monolog finally ended, the officers shook the water off the furniture and carried it back into the house. It was never again seen outside.

Eventually, Aunt Anna cooled down and told everyone that these Americans were really very nice *boys*. They had been thoughtless, as boys are wont to be, but not the least bit arrogant. After all, the conquerors did not *have* to let an old German woman lecture them. They could have simply shoved her aside, she knew.

In April 1945, the owners of *our* villa returned to Kempen. This represented a serious dilemma since they quite naturally demanded to live in their property again, while we were unwilling to camp in the street. After a few days of cramped coexistence, the problem was solved by the American authorities who allowed us to move back into the upstairs of our home. The officers continued to stay below.

The washhouse had been converted into an army kitchen. There the soldiers prepared copious meals on a fire-spewing contraption that bore closer resemblance to a flamethrower than to a cooking stove. A red-hot, hissing stream of fire shot forth from its nozzle into a long channel made from two rows of brick on which sat the pots and pans with their delectable contents.

I had not set eyes on so much food in years. For breakfast, dozens of eggs and bacon or sausages swam in a sea of fat. For lunch or dinner, a blend of onions and heaps of canned meat simmered in rancid oil that splattered over floor and walls, all this accompanied by mounds of bread whiter than any I had ever seen. The penetrating odor, and especially the abundant quantities, seemed divine to me, nourishment fit for the gods. But the officers accepted their fare with an indifference bordering on aversion. Clearly, they did not think of themselves as immortals feasting on heavenly ambrosia.

Once, after I had traded three pounds of ripe strawberries from our garden for an American ham, Mother and Aunt Anna fixed a mouthwatering treat for us—tender, juicy ham with plums, *Reibekuchen* (German potato pancakes) and fresh peas. The aroma proved irresistible to one of the officers. He knocked on the kitchen door, inhaled the fragrant air with a beatific smile, and proposed that henceforth he would supply food for all of us if Mother and Aunt Anna agreed to invite him and his friends for dinner.

The bargain was quickly struck. We lived well for the next three weeks, sharing the harvest of our garden with our *house guests* and eating their plentiful army provisions. The pounds we gained in that brief span were to stand us in good stead later when we returned to Aachen and had to survive entirely on our pitiful rations.

Unfortunately, the American unit in Kempen was soon moved to another part of Germany across the Rhine. It was with some genuine regret—and not just because we had lost our providers—that we saw them go. Even Aunt Anna had become fond of the *boys*.

By the time they left, my English had improved noticeably. I could make the soldiers understand most of what I wanted to say, and if they spoke slowly, I could actually grasp the meaning of their words. On several occasions, I acted as their interpreter to facilitate a trade between them and a local farmer: cigarettes for fresh asparagus or coffee for a piglet. Sometimes, they let me climb into a tank. Standing proudly in the hatch, I saw my friends turn green with envy as we rode through the streets of Kempen. Even Leonore was greatly impressed by my flashy pose.

Obviously, living under occupation was not half as bad as I had been led to believe.

CHAPTER 22

Democracy had been a dirty word in the Third Reich. Now, it was on everybody's lips. According to the new Gospel, it was a blessed form of government, in sharp contrast to the accursed nature of the Führer's autocratic rule. The evil of the Nazi state and its disastrous consequences had become plain to me, but of democracy, I knew nothing before the officers billeted with us explained what it meant: a government deriving its powers from the people, equality of opportunity, and respect for the dignity and the rights of every individual.

It seemed like a good system to me. I eagerly waited to see it in action. A first object lesson was soon provided.

One morning, the rumble of powerful engines drew me from my work in the garden. I got to the gate just as dozens of heavy Army trucks pulled up by the castle and spilled out a battalion of black soldiers who were to take the place of the departing Americans. In disbelief, I stared at the exotic sight.

Up to then, my information about Negroes had been, with one exception, entirely second- or even thirdhand. My earliest recollection went back to the profound regret I had always felt upon finishing a *Mohrenkopf* (moors head), a delicious chocolate-covered cream puff, which used to be a favorite of mine in the happy days when food was plentiful and the cafés still served their infinite variety of pastries. In just a few bites, a sweet-toothed cannibal like me had gobbled up the whole head, leaving nothing but rich, sticky chocolate smudges on my lips and cheeks. Oh, how I had wished that *moors* had bigger heads.

Later, I learned from my picture books all about Black tribes-men living in the happy hunting grounds of Africa's primeval forests. I remember especially one illustration showing three Black boys and an elephant. When I pulled a tab at the bottom, the pachyderm's wrinkled trunk flipped up from the page, and the two naked fig-ures on its back hopped up and down while the third, incongruously clothed in red bathing trunks, raised his prod to goad the animal on its way. And how could I ever forget that memorable episode in *Struwwelpeter* (*Slovenly Peter*), a popular illustrated children's book, where three boys are punished for making fun of a *kohlpechraben-schwarzer Mohr* (coal pitch raven black moor) by being dunked into an inkwell from which they emerged as black as their victim.

Only once had I actually seen a Negro, or rather two, in person. That was in the summer of 1938. We were taking a cruise on the Rhine River. Suddenly, I spied a white suit and in it, a gentleman whose face shone like burnished ebony. He was talking to a lady wearing a blue silk dress, her skin as light as a carved Madonna. I fixed my eyes on these spell-binding apparitions with far more won-der than I felt for the fairy-tale castles drifting by on the slopes of the Rhine Valley.

A rude tug at my sleeve interrupted my unabashed staring. Father pulled me away, lifting his hat in an apologetic greeting to the couple, who acknowledged his action with a smile. Thereafter, I had to content myself with looking discreetly, from a distance, at the fascinating sight from another world.

Such then was my knowledge of Blacks when a whole battalion of them took up their quarters in the castle across from our house. My curiosity about Negroes was, of course, far from satisfied by the single encounter on the riverboat years ago. So I quickly dropped my work and walked over to the trucks, hoping for a chance to strike up a conversation with one of the men as I watched them unload their gear.

A few of the Black soldiers began throwing candy to the little boys and girls playing in the park grounds by the castle. The giv-ing proved contagious, and soon the Americans were outdoing each other until their supplies of sweets were exhausted. It was hard to tell who got more joy from this display of generosity: the soldiers, who beamed all over at the squeals of delight, or the children, who slowly savored every bite of the rare candy.

I stood aside, observing the scene. Chocolate would taste good, I admitted to myself, but I thought it a bit undignified at my age to scramble for candy in the company of these *toddlers*. Hermann, however, had no such scruples. He got hold of a handful of sweets and offered me part of a Hershey bar, thus saving me from the painful dilemma of having to choose between my pride and my hankering for chocolate.

Two army cars stopped in front of our house. Four White officers knocked on the door and presented their papers to Uncle Anton. They must be our new tenants who—we had been told—would take over the rooms vacated by their compatriots. The Black drivers carried the baggage inside and then joined their comrades at the castle. Suddenly, it dawned on me that there were no officers, only some corporals and sergeants, among the hundreds of Negroes I had seen arrive in our town.

The soldiers gradually disappeared behind the walls. Hermann and I headed back home. It seemed unlikely we would get to know any of them that day.

Our relationship with the two captains and the two lieutenants quartered in our house was limited to an occasional perfunctory greeting if our paths crossed in the hallway. They took their meals at a restaurant which had been requisitioned and turned into an officers' club by the occupation forces. Black soldiers did the cooking and waited on the tables.

Uncle Anton had been in America on a business trip during prohibition. He explained what he knew about race relations in the United States. Blacks and Whites did not mix much. They went to different schools, lived in different neighborhoods, and held different jobs. Negroes worked as busboys, porters, street cleaners, servants, and laborers. There were many laws curtailing (*"beschneiden"* was the German word Uncle Anton used) their rights.

"You mean," I asked, "Blacks in America are like Jews here in Germany under Hitler?"

"No, it's not nearly as bad as that. At one time, they were bought and sold like cattle, but slavery ended some eighty years ago. And I imagine life has improved for them since my visit."

I mulled these things over in my mind. Uncle Anton's words seemed strangely at odds with what I had learned about democracy from the first group of officers who had stayed with us.

One day, Hermann came home bubbling with excitement. He had made friends with Joseph, a Black sergeant from Chicago. Joseph had taken him for a ride in a jeep to a nearby army depot and shown him pictures of his wife and two children. Tomorrow, my brother promised he would introduce me to him.

In preparation for this encounter, I pulled out my German-English dictionary to memorize some useful terms for an interview I intended to conduct. Certainly I would need the English equivalent of the German word *Neger*. The book provided two choices: negro and nigger. I liked the sound of the second better and added it to my vocabulary. How was a thirteen-year-old boy to know that the abbreviation *pej.* printed after the word stood for *pejorative* and that pejorative meant the expression had a disparaging, negative connotation?

Next, I looked up the word for *beschneiden* and found a long list of entries: cut, pare, trim, circumcise, curtail, and reduce. Of all these, *circumcise* struck me as the most impressive verb.

Thus equipped, Hermann and I set out for the castle. At the entrance, my brother asked for Sergeant Joseph from Chicago. Soon, he appeared and led us into a room he shared with several other soldiers. We gave him some strawberries we had picked that morning. He dipped one into a bowl of sugar, smacked his lips, and then called on his comrades to join him. Quickly, they ate the few berries, thanking us as profusely as if we had brought a royal gift.

Hermann left with one of the men for another excursion in a jeep. I wanted to see Joseph's family pictures. Two girls, five and three years old, played in a little garden in front of a white frame house. A plump, pleasant-looking woman held on to her windblown kerchief by the shore of a lake. And there was Joseph standing on a scaffolding and wearing a helmet. "I am a construction foreman in Chicago," he said.

I was curious to question him about democracy in America. "Are the rights of niggers circumcised in your country?" I asked, flaunting my newly acquired vocabulary.

A tense silence fell over the room. The soldiers, who had been so friendly a short while ago, glowered at me. Had I done something wrong? I felt a threat hanging in the air and instinctively stepped back, afraid that one of them was about to hit me.

Joseph waved him aside. "Where did you get the word?"

"What word?"

"Nigger."

"In this dictionary." I had brought it along just in case I should need it to make myself understood. Joseph showed no interest in it. "Are you sure you did not learn it from the officers in your house?" he asked.

I answered truthfully that I had not spoken a single sentence to them. Joseph appeared relieved. He took my dictionary. "No good," he said, "no good this book. That's a bad word. Don't ever use it again."

The soldiers relaxed sensing that I had meant no insult. Joseph began answering my questions. Democracy was only for Whites, he explained. Yes, he was earning pretty good money. No, there was no such thing as equality of opportunity. Yes, all his neighbors were Black, and his children would go to an all Black school. No, the law didn't treat Negroes and Whites the same way.

Joseph laid out the shortcomings of democracy in a matter-of-fact tone of voice, without bitterness, it seemed to me. But when he spoke of the future, he was a man possessed by a vision. "Things are going to change," he declared with prophetic assurance. "We won't be stepped on any longer. We'll take what's rightfully ours. One way or another, by God, we'll *take* it." His comrades, who had been listening with as much interest as I, shouted their approval, "Yes, Joseph, we'll take it! Ain't nobody can keep it from us."

Every time I referred to the *circumcised* rights of Negroes, Joseph laughed. "That from your dictionary, too?" he asked at last. When I nodded, he added, "Well, it's no good, no good. Better throw it away." And he tossed my precious book into a corner from where I later stealthily retrieved it.

Now it was Joseph's turn to put questions to me. Why did we Germans hate the Jews so much? Why had we killed millions of them in our gas chambers?

I had witnessed the *Kristallnacht*. I had heard speeches about Jewish greed and treachery. I knew about the *Rassengesetze* (racial laws) and about trains taking Jews to special camps, but this was the first time anybody had ever mentioned gas chambers to me. Millions killed? I did not know of even a single Jew having been killed. Surely, Joseph was wrong, duped by the propaganda of war, just as we had been deceived by vicious lies from our government. No, this could not have happened, not in Germany.

My words spilled out heatedly, ungrammatically, incoherently. What I lacked in eloquence I made up for in steadfastness of conviction. Joseph sadly shook his head. It was all true, he insisted. All this had really happened.

At night, I brought the subject up at home. Both Father and Uncle Anton said they did not know exactly what had been done to the Jews, but they feared we would soon learn of horrible crimes. Indeed, as the weeks passed, we saw evidence of atrocities beyond human imagination. Report after report documented the unspeakable brutality of the concentration camps. And always, there were the dreadful pictures. Pictures of ghastly survivors who looked like skeletons from the grave, of aseptic gas chambers, and of piles of corpses. They engraved themselves deep in my heart, rising in the darkness to march through the doomed world of my nightmares.

I did not have the strength to pursue to the end this crushing catalog of cruelties, yet I understood now that the Germany I had been so proud of not long ago had become a hell upon earth.

Some people disputed the figures contained in this reckoning of horrors. They claimed the statistics exaggerated. Not five or six, but *only* one or two million Jews had been killed.

Father had the right answer for this shabby arithmetic of death. "Two million, six million," he said, "there is no *real* difference. They are both infinite, beyond comprehension. Even if only one million had been murdered, our guilt would not be one iota less."

Years later, I read the *Diary of Anne Frank*. She died when she was just a little older than I was in this spring of 1945. Strange that her frail voice should have outlived the savage chorus of hatred and violence which rent the skies of her and my childhood. I think it was she who finally took away my nightmares. "It is a miracle," she wrote, "that I have not yet given up all hope... But I hold fast to it, despite everything, because *I still believe in the good of man.*"

CHAPTER 23

In the evening, a bevy of young women on bicycles used to arrive at the *Burg*. Most of them came from the city of Krefeld, less than an hour's ride away. They would walk around the castle as if admiring its neo-Gothic architecture. Impressive though the structure might be, I could not help being amazed at the suddenness with which it had been turned into a major tourist attraction. After all, a sixteen-mile round trip, just to see this building, seemed excessive, especially in view of the severe food shortage which made any unnecessary exertion ill-advised.

The mystery of the foolish virgins on bicycles was soon solved. In fact, they were neither foolish nor virgins. After a brief inspection of the outside of the castle, they were invariably invited by some Black soldiers to a guided tour of the interior. This would last anywhere from twenty minutes to several hours. From time to time, a few of the women, their handbags bulging at the seams, emerged from the building to mount their bicycles, which they had chained to a tree or post in the park. No doubt, they were carrying home the reward for their labors, precious provisions, such as canned meat, bread, butter, chocolate, coffee, and cigarettes. I began to understand that the energy balance, weighing the effort of both the journey and the activities performed inside the *Burg* against the dietary improvement represented by the treasures stuffed into the bags, came out decidedly positive.

The good people of Kempen did not approve of these nighttime visits to the castle, and their righteous anger was kindled by a fiery sermon preached in the church of *Sankt Katharina*, which had the misfortune of opening onto the *Burg* park and thus having to witness the nocturnal comings and goings. The priest thundered against the *shameful vice,* and *profligate sinfulness* perpetrated by these *godless* women. I found his outspoken moral indignation that Sunday strangely at odds with the discreet silence that had shrouded the mass murder of the Jews throughout my years of regular church attendance.

A group of neighborhood boys decided to stamp out the evil denounced by the priest. Some, perhaps, saw themselves as instruments of the divine will while others may have been simply envious of the soldiers who so easily obtained what they themselves only dreamed of. Still others had nothing in mind but to play a practical joke on the ladies of the night. And so the guardians of public morality, the jealous, and the pranksters together hatched a plot. They were going to puncture all the bicycle tires. Then some of the boys would shadow their victims, hooting and taunting them on their long walk back to Krefeld. Though I, too, was saddened by the sale of bodies for a mess of pottage, I declined an invitation to take part in the scheme. Who knows how desperately—and for whom—these women needed the food obtained in exchange for their favors?

At any rate, the plotters had reckoned without Joseph. When he heard of the cyclists' plight, he refused to let them trudge through the night to Krefeld. Instead, he loaded the women and their bikes onto an army truck and drove off to the city. Unfortunately for him, he had a little accident on the way back. Fatigue, a generous consumption of whiskey, and the bad condition of the roads caused him to slide into a ditch where an MP patrol found him singing to the moon.

I learned all of this a few days later from Joseph, who was doing time behind a barred window of a basement dungeon in the *Burg*. He would have to spend a little while there, he informed me cheerfully. In the evening, when some female visitors appeared, careful this time to take their bicycles into the castle's entrance hall, I heard his beautiful baritone intone the words *Joshua fit the battle of Jericho, Jericho, Jericho. Joshua fit the battle of Jericho, and the walls came tumbling down.* Soon, they did come tumbling down. Joseph was free again.

Chapter 24

One day, a little boy was climbing up and down our garden gate. The tank crew had rammed one of the stone pillars to which the gate was hinged. All at once, it came crashing down, forcing the child's head through the narrow space between two iron bars. A horrible scream pierced the air. Scraped flesh hung from both sides of the boy's face. His ears dangled loosely from the bloody cheeks.

We ran out to help him as he lay crushed beneath the weight of the gate, but our efforts to lift it up and pull it over his head proved of no avail. He could not bear the pain of the bars pressing against his raw skin. At last, Aunt Anna remembered that up to the age of six, a child's body can pass through the same width as the head. She turned the boy until his shoulders were lined up parallel to the bars and then directed us to pull him up. It worked.

I rushed into the street to flag down a German driver who was just going by our house. The hospital was only a couple of minutes away—would he please take the boy there? The man saw the blood spilling all over the child's clothes and onto the ground, mumbled something about the spotless, beige upholstery in his *Opel,* and sped off—in the direction of the hospital.

Father raised his walking cane in a gesture of impotent rage. For the first time in my life, I heard a profanity—"*du gottverfluchtes Schwein*"—issue from his lips. We were all disgusted but had no time then to reflect on the morals of a man who valued clean upholstery above human life. Mother and Uncle Anton tried to stop the bleeding with a makeshift bandage, while Aunt Anna wrapped the shivering victim in a blanket.

Screeching brakes in front of our house. An army jeep. In it Joseph and Hermann, who had had the presence of mind to run to the *Burg* and get our new American friend. A moment later, Aunt Anna, cradling the boy in her arms, and Joseph were off to the hospital. Surely, I said to myself, as I saw the jeep disappear in the distance, Joseph would have taken the child in his own car, even if it were brand-new, without worrying about bloodstains on the seats.

When Aunt Anna came home, she had good news. The doctors believed they could heal the boy's wounds and reattach his torn ears. She told us she had invited Joseph for dinner but was not certain he had understood her. Since she spoke no English, that fear seemed well-founded, and so Hermann and I went over to the castle to confirm the dinner date for next evening.

Mother and Aunt Anna had prepared a rare feast: white asparagus with cold-sliced eggs but without the traditional ham which was not to be had anywhere. For the main course one of our illegal chickens had been sacrificed, and for dessert, we had cherries from our garden.

Joseph did not mention Jews or racial problems that night. He talked about his life in Chicago, his work as a construction foreman, and his family. He passed the pictures, which Hermann and I had already seen, around the table and proudly showed us a letter, scrawled in a child's awkward, big handwriting: "We miss you, Daddy. Hugs and kisses, Bessie." It was the first letter his daughter had ever penned in her own hand.

Before he left, Joseph gave some chocolate to Marita, Hermann, and me. To Mother and Aunt Anna, he handed a can of coffee. Nothing could have pleased them more, for their long-standing consumption of *Ersatzkaffee*, far from inuring them to its dreary taste, had become a constant reminder that once upon a time they had known the heavenly aroma of real coffee.

On the way out, just as we were all saying goodbye to him, Joseph ran into the American officers billeted with us. They were returning home for the night. Why did they stare at him as if he were a specter out of the netherworld? Joseph saluted smartly, waved at us, and sauntered across the street into the park.

Next morning, the officers demanded to see Uncle Anton. "Don't ever invite any of the Negro soldiers into your house, again," they ordered.

CHAPTER 25

In May of 1945, the war in Europe ended. The Führer had killed himself amid the convulsive *Götterdämmerung* of his one-thousand-year Reich. Though not yet fourteen years old, by Hitler's reckoning, I had surpassed the age of Methuselah since I was born five and a half months before the Nazis came to power and was still alive when the Third Reich collapsed. And in truth, I felt as if I had lived thousand years. So full of history had my times been, full of horror and hope, of hatred and love, of lies and idealism, and of nightmares and dreams.

Father was getting impatient to return to Aachen. Unwilling to wait for trains or buses to resume service, he decided that he and I should go by bicycle to see if we could find a place to stay for our family in the devastated city. There was just one hitch: he had not been on a bicycle since his childhood days and, to make matters worse, bore in his left leg a permanent memento of World War I in the form of a painful machine gun wound.

I started giving lessons to Father in the little courtyard behind the house, for he refused adamantly to practice on the streets of Kempen, perhaps because he feared for his dignity. What would people think to see him pedal a wobbly course on the Burgring, with his son in hot pursuit, trying to stem the gravity-defying tilt of a bike ridden by an elderly gentleman wearing a well-used but neat suit plus vest, tie, and hat. I must add here that my father never went outside without these accoutrements just as a turtle never ventures forth without the protective armor of its shell. Father was not about to make an exception for his bicycle training.

Thus, we practiced in the narrow confines of the courtyard. There was no straight stretch anywhere, nothing but an unending, continuous curve which, of course, made the whole exercise that much more difficult. Father's stiff left leg would not bend. Most of the time, it dragged along the pavement lending support to his precarious equilibrium. His sound leg worked for two but still managed to maintain no more than the minimum forward motion, which I did my best to boost through breathless pushing. My steadying hand could not prevent a bad fall as Father crashed into the wall of the washhouse. Mother tried frantically to dissuade him from any further efforts. He would not listen. After an hour's recuperation, he was back on his bike. Only a second spill and two hopelessly stiff legs next morning put an end to his—and my—exertions.

I breathed a sigh of relief. Our chances of successfully maneuvering the sixty miles from Kempen to Aachen had not appeared promising to me, and what would I have done if we had broken down somewhere in the middle of nowhere?

In July, the first trains started running again. I was terribly disappointed when Father announced I would have to stay behind with Marita and Hermann. Mother and he were going to Aachen to look for a place to stay.

Tears in my eyes as I waved goodbye to my parents as they fought their way into an overcrowded cattle car that was to take them to Krefeld. There they hoped to pick up another train to continue their journey.

A week later, Father and Mother returned, depressed about what they had seen, yet happy to have found an apartment though they described it as only barely habitable. Still, it would give us the shelter we needed and allow us to rebuild our lives in Aachen.

The pleasant interlude at Kempen was over. A harsh reality was awaiting us, but we were all eager to go home.

Chapter 26

Marita, Hermann, and I rode in back of a borrowed truck amid the furniture and bedding, the pots and pans which our relatives had given us to help us get started. The trip was slow. More than once, we were forced to detour through fields or pastures around bomb craters in the road. As we approached Aachen, my heart beat wildly with joy. This was the moment I had been waiting for. This was home—forgotten were Uncle Anton and Aunt Anna, forgotten Leonore and Joseph, forgotten the easy life at Kempen. There we had been marking time. Here we had work to do. I felt like a bear coming out of hibernation, blood flowing with renewed vitality at winter's end.

In the distance, I could make out the cathedral's dome and choir and its pseudo-Gothic steeple, whose stolid form had always offended my sense of aesthetics. It would have been nice if a shell had shaved it off without, of course, destroying the rest of the great church. The medieval town hall, too, was still there though its two towers were gone. Much of Aachen resembled an expanse of ruins, more desolate even than what I remembered, but perhaps it was just that my eyes were no longer used to such sweeping devastation after the year at Kempen.

Later, I explored the city whenever I had time, looking for friends and familiar landmarks. The streets were still choked with rubble. Some sections were utterly leveled. Here and there, clusters of houses rose up from the wasteland, and they were teeming with life, for every day, thousands of citizens were coming home. The clanging of shovels and pickaxes filled the air as the male population over sixteen fulfilled its duty to clear away rubble three times a week. Among the gray and ragged workers, I found many I knew. I often lent a helping hand myself, but it seemed all so futile. I could not imagine that in my lifetime, Aachen would ever return to normal again.

Certainly our lodgings were far from normal. When the truck stopped in the Saarstrasse, at the foot of the Salvatorberg, we children ran into the house to inspect our new quarters—three rooms plus a kitchen on the ground floor, no windowpanes, of course, but unexpectedly, a gaping hole in the wall between the front room and the hallway. There was no bathroom. The five of us had to go across the hallway to use the toilet of another family. Formerly, the whole ground floor had been a single apartment. Now, because two-thirds of the buildings in Aachen had been destroyed, the city government rationed all rooms. In fact, we had to thank Father's World War I injury and a doctor's testimony that he needed a sickroom, for permission to keep this sumptuous half of an apartment for ourselves without being obliged to share it with an additional tenant.

We settled into a new routine. Running water had not yet been restored to our district, so Hermann and I became water carriers. A few minutes from our house was a public faucet. There we would wait in line with other members of the neighborhood's water brigade, fill our buckets, and take them home. It was amazing how much water our family needed on an ordinary day, but on washday, it was as if we were moving an entire ocean to Mother's kitchen. Our arms and shoulders hurt so badly that we recommended to her—in vain, of course—to let us all wear dirty clothes and do our laundry maybe twice a year, but she did reward us for our toil with an extra liverwurst sandwich or a piece of cake.

These were a few of her incredible culinary creations, for the *liverwurst* contained absolutely no meat yet managed to remind us, however faintly, of the real thing. I still wonder how she did it. Her *cake*, made from potatoes and elderberries, looked remarkably like a genuine cake instead of the counterfeit it was.

Elderberries had become Mother's favorite cooking ingredient. She knew every tree within miles and served us an endless diet of elderberry soups, dumplings, and puddings. Much to her disappointment, we ate these concoctions with less and less enthusiasm, proving once and for all that, even when hungry, man does not live by elderberries alone.

On the rare occasions the family decided to take a bath, Hermann and I were faced with some difficult choices. We could collect enough wood on the Salvatorberg or among the ruins to stoke up a fire and thus bring the temperature of the cold water from the public faucet up to lukewarm. Or we would get water from one of the city's many hot sulfur springs. That would save us the trouble of fetching wood but meant lugging our buckets twice as far, all the way from the *Quellenhof*, a former luxury hotel. Mother had taught us how to swim in its thermal pool before we were five years old. So we knew the place well, yet it was hardly recognizable now. In the battle for Aachen, the hotel had served as the last command post for the German defenders. It had been pounded relentlessly by American artillery fire, but its sorry present condition had not kept homeless squatters from occupying every square inch still fit for human habitation. Oven pipes jutted through the windows. From a line strung between the sides of a particularly large breach in the facade, white bed sheets flapped in the wind as if signaling surrender.

After the choice between getting hot water from the Quellenhof or cold water from the public faucet, an even more irksome dilemma confronted my brother and me. First, Mother and Father took their baths in the big tin tub placed in the center of the kitchen for the event. Then we could either dump the water and fill the tub all over again, which entailed a good couple of hours of work, or bravely step into the increasingly thick and turbid liquid with the result that the hapless fifth and last bather emerged from the ordeal by water no cleaner than he had been before.

Fortunately, this state of affairs did not last long. The water mains were repaired, and in 1946, a public bath reopened. There you could wait your turn to take a shower in double quick time, for the water was metered and ruthlessly shut off once you had used up your allotted amount. Have you ever been caught covered with soap and no way to rinse it off? I haven't either. I learned to be fast in the shower.

There was just one high school left in Aachen, and it had room for upper-level students only. So we had plenty of free time, especially when the water chores ended. Hermann and I began digging among the ruins of our old house in the Grosskölnstrasse. We tried to remember exactly where the trapdoor in the backyard had been. If we could find it, we might be able to penetrate into the basement and recover some of the treasures stored there. After moving mountains of rubble, we finally hit pay dirt. Never had I heard a more beautiful sound than the metallic clang of my shovel striking the steel door. We had caught a small corner of it on the very first attempt.

Next morning, we continued our excavations with redoubled vigor until the entire trapdoor was exposed. Though it was bent out of shape, we managed to pry it open. Carefully we went underground, shining a flashlight ahead to see if it was safe to go on. The massive vaults, which had protected us in so many air raids, looked solid enough except in one place where the ceiling buckled in a menacing arc crisscrossed by cracks of a finger's breadth.

Hermann and I sped past this danger spot straight to Father's wine cellar. There it was, untouched, row upon row of bottles neatly stacked on their shelves. What a treasure trove we had come upon! This wine would be worth a fortune in trade. Two *Graacher Himmelreich* for a sack of potatoes or one *Schloss Eltz* for a ham.

First, however, we were going to take our finder's reward. Confident that Father's meticulously accurate wine list had gone up in smoke along with our other possessions, we decided we could, with impunity, indulge in a sampling of the golden liquid. We opened a *Kröver Nacktarsch*, chiefly because the label, showing a little boy with a bare bottom, intrigued us. It tasted good, and being thirsty from the day's work, we uncorked a second bottle. A delicious feeling of drowsiness and relaxation descended on our tired bodies. We sat down on a damp straw mattress and floated off into a world of happy dreams.

Suddenly I was shaken by a firm hand. In Noah's time, it was the son who surprised his father, lying drunken and naked in his tent. Here the roles were reversed: Father stumbled, quite literally, upon his drunk, though not naked sons snoozing in the catacombs beneath our bombed-out house. He had become worried when we failed to return from our excavations at the usual time for lunch and set forth to look for us. But where Noah had cast a curse upon Ham, Father did not even rebuke us.

"We must move all these bottles out of here today," he said to me. "Hurry up and get the wheelbarrow. You and Hermann transport the wine to the Saarstrasse while I stand guard here."

Seven trips later, all one hundred and sixty-two bottles were safely in our apartment. We had beaten the 10:30 p.m. curfew by half an hour. That night, we felt immeasurably richer: with our new-found wealth, we could look confidently into the future.

I fell into bed dead tired. It had been a hard day's work, but how much more satisfying it was to haul wine instead of water. I praised the Lord for having wrought this latter-day version of the miracle of Cana.

CHAPTER 27

When we arrived in the Grosskölnstrasse next morning, we were amazed to find the trapdoor open. We had left it closed and covered with a layer of rubble to disguise the entrance to the basement, which still held a winter's worth of coal. Hermann and I rushed into the storage room. The pile of coal had visibly shrunk. No doubt, a freebooter had been at work here since the end of the nighttime curfew at 4:30 a.m. He must have observed yesterday's unusual activity and concluded that still other treasures might be hidden beneath the trapdoor.

There was just one way to prevent any further losses. One of us would have to be on guard duty at all times, while the other carted away the coal. For two days, Hermann and I took turns defending the basement and pushing loaded wheelbarrows, always uphill, to our apartment in the Saarstrasse, with time off only during curfew hours. It was worth the effort. We did not freeze that winter.

Though we were doing coal miner's work, we did not receive any extra food rations, to which all people in strenuous occupations were entitled. Everything was controlled then: living space, socks, shoes, clothing, kilowatt-hours, and worst of all, food. When in 1946 our already pitiful rations were twice more reduced, our distress erupted into noisy hunger demonstrations throughout the city.

I remember one dinner when I stared at a minute portion of beef on my plate, aware that this would be the only meat for some time. "May I have a little more, Mother," I pleaded. Silently Mother continued filling the other plates. No, she did not fill them. She put a few mouthfuls on each. There was nothing left. Her own plate was the emptiest of all. Then, with a painful look, she took a knife and cut my four small cubes into eight tiny pieces. I never again asked for more than my share.

Naturally, the black market flourished in those years, but Father wanted nothing to do with it. Food was scarce, and it was not right to feast at the expense of other starving people. We all had to make an equal sacrifice and share what little there was. Even when his business reopened, in emergency quarters and on a far smaller scale than before, and he had sheets, towels, drapes, tablecloths, lingerie, and fabrics for sale, all rationed of course, he agreed to an illegal trade of his merchandise on only one or two occasions and then with extreme reluctance. He did it for his hungry children. He himself refused to eat any of the ill-gotten food from the black market.

In desperation, Mother conceived the most unexpected and ingenious survival techniques. She would walk into a bakeshop, order two loaves of bread, and strike up a scintillating, nonstop conversation with the baker or his wife. Never at a loss for a topic, she complimented *her* on a blouse, stirred up *his* ire at some political issue, inquired about their children, discussed the latest soccer match, about which she knew absolutely nothing, or talked about the weather, a famous psychic's prophesies for the future, or the arrival of thousands of refugees expelled from their homelands in Germany's eastern provinces. In the middle of her performance, she would put the money for the bread on the counter, continue her palaver for an astutely calculated period of time, and then make her exit—without handing over any of her ration coupons. The baker and his wife were left lost in admiration of her eloquence or, perhaps, cursing her loquacity. Either way, Mother was happy so long as she succeeded in talking them out of a loaf or two.

More than once, I saw her pull off this trick in each of the three shops she patronized, and more than once, I saw her get caught. It did not embarrass her in the least. With a breezy, "How would I be so absentminded?" she gave up the precious coupons, added a few minutes of chatter for good measure, and walked out, still a valued customer.

On Sundays, the whole family went to Holy Mass. Most of the churches had been destroyed in bombing raids during the war. The few that had survived unscathed were always overcrowded. Maybe we all felt the need to do penance and return to God after the aberrations of the Hitler years. The pews were reserved for the old and wounded. We young folk stood in the aisles, tightly packed together.

I was quite undernourished at that time. All my growing was vertical. A photograph of the period shows a lanky, tall, emaciated youth with an ascetic appearance about him and a rib cage exhibiting each arched bone as clearly as the skeleton in the high school science lab. Even today, I am seized by compassion when I contemplate the picture of this pitiful figure that was I.

Several times, I had fainted in the claustrophobic atmosphere of the church crowded to suffocation. It was a strange experience: Candles began to dance in fiery circles. Windows closed in on me with blinding light. Columns metamorphosed into sinuous curves along the swaying nave, and the sea of worshippers swelled and subsided like a wave breaking on a rocky shore. Everything swirled and spun, went out of focus, and then vanished into night. I must have fallen down, utterly weak, unable to move, yet dimly aware that I was being picked up and walked down the aisle to the vestry. Curiously, I did not catch the sound of the footsteps of those supporting me, though my own reverberated like hammer blows in a long tunnel. I was placed on a chair. Someone moistened my temples. I heard the anxious voices of the good Samaritans attending me without understanding what they were saying. At last, I came to, startled by what had happened to me.

In spite of such experiences, I did not lose a sense of cautious optimism. True, quite a few people had been killed stepping on mines or setting off other explosives since our return to Aachen, but the frequency of these fatal accidents was dropping rapidly. Most of the city still lay in ruins, but it was an orderly wasteland now. The rubble had been cleared off the streets and carted away to designated dumping grounds. Food remained scarce, but our stomach shrank and got used to smaller portions. Everybody could freely speak his mind without fear of denunciation. Municipal services had been restored. Our orchestra gave its first concert in an unheated gymnasium, and in the spring of 1946, the rebuilt foyer of the bombed-out *Stadttheater* reopened with Schiller's *Don Carlos*.

At night, still under the spell of the poet's passionate language, I lay awake thinking about the tragedy. I kept remembering what the Marquis de Posa had said to Phillip II:

> Sire, man is more than you may think of him,
> And he will break the chains of this long night
> To claim again his innate, sacred right.

Did not these words apply with equal force to our time? Yes, we *were* more than Hitler had made of us, and darkness *had* given way to a new day. The chains were broken.

CHAPTER 28

One morning, Mother asked me to hang up some wet laundry in the loft. I climbed up the stairs and, passing the tiny WC right next to the attic room, felt an irrepressible need to use it. I turned the door handle. Somebody was holding it from inside. Instead of the usual *besetzt* (occupied), however, I heard mellow baritone intone, *"O du mein holder Abendstern"* ("O thou sublime, sweet evening star") from Wagner's *Tannhäuser*. This was no ordinary voice. I myself had been wont to sing in the bathroom when we still had one to ourselves, but how feeble my efforts had been compared to this glorious voice that sang through the entire aria with breathtaking beauty and style.

At last the door opened. A rotund, middle-aged man in a purple robe stood before me. His velvety baritone had made me forget temporarily why I had stopped in front of his WC. Suddenly, the elementary urge reasserted itself. I rushed inside almost before I had asked, "Herr von Eschenbach," as I called him, for permission to use it.

He did not mind. In fact, he burst out laughing, "So you know I was singing the part of Wolfram von Eschenbach?" he said. "You must love opera to know your way about so well."

Thus, it was that I made Herr Jussen's—that was his *real* name—acquaintance. He had received an appointment at the Aachen opera company and moved into the attic room of our house. Among the many things I learned from him, the most surprising was that opera singing passed for a strenuous occupation and that singers with leading parts therefore got extra food rations just like stokers and coalminers.

I would have taken up voice training myself had it not been for my former music teacher's scathing comment that I sang like a frog, which made it appear unlikely I would ever land a major part. But though I was envious, I did not begrudge our singers their dietary supplement. Who had ever heard a big voice come from a spindly body. Besides, Herr Jussen assured me it took tremendous physical stamina to get through *Die Meistersinger* or *Der Rosenkavalier*, and didn't the hungry audience need music even more desperately than another bite to eat? I agreed.

At any rate, there was a far more foolproof way to fill my stomach than to prepare for an operatic career. Together with Marita and Hermann, I would go *hamstering*. This newly-coined verb aptly describes what people were doing: scour the countryside, beg or barter for food, stuff it in pouches, and carry it home as a provision for a rainy day. A *rainy day*, of course, was every day, no matter how brightly the sun might be shining.

Our destination was the village of Lövenich, where Father had grown up. Like other rural towns, it had a look of prosperity about it. Persian rugs covered the floors of the farmhouses. Silver tea services glittered on many a sideboard, and the farmer's wives sported diamond rings on their callous hands used to hard work. All these things had been acquired from townsfolk, who were trading whatever valuables they had left for bacon, eggs, and flour.

We did not need to offer anything in exchange although, at Father's insistence, we forced some bottles of wine on his childhood companions. I was unable, however, to force any farmer to accept the gift of an operatic aria I had prepared, with Herr Jussen's assistance, as a token of my gratitude for the expected dole of food. No sooner had I uttered the first phrase *"Alles fühlt der Liebe Freuden"* ("All feel the tender joys of love") than they all took to their heels pleading some chore that required their immediate attention. Perhaps, I did sound like a frog after all. Chastened by the experience, I soon gave up singing for good.

Apart from this musical fiasco, we were welcomed with open arms as soon as we mentioned our names. And as our hosts fed us pea soup with big chunks of sausage, or fresh bread with butter and ham, or heaps of potatoes with onions and eggs, or plum cake with whipped cream, they began talking about their youthful adventures. One remembered the time Father had hitched his Saint Bernard to a sled and taken him on a wild ride down the village street. Another still shook with laughter when he thought about the honey dropping onto the schoolmaster's bald head from a hot stone suspended precisely above his desk. A third remembered how Father had stolen the model student's clothes at the local swimming hole. The embarrassed victim had waited until dark to sneak home, uncovered and undiscovered, or so he hoped. But a gang of boys had lain in ambush and made such a racket with their pots and pans that half the population hung from their windows, just in time to catch sight of the naked fellow bathed in the glow of numerous torches.

A few of the men had gone to the gymnasium in the next town. They had not forgotten the long walks—an hour and a quarter each way—they had shared with Father for several years. Grandfather would not buy his son a bicycle since the other parents in Lövenich could not afford one for their children, but when the weather was really bad, he ordered the business carriage to be got ready and had the coachman drive all the students to school.

With so many people having fond recollections of Father, our hamstering expeditions always turned out successful, too successful almost, for it was forbidden to carry more food than could legally have been obtained with ration coupons. If you were caught, the contraband would be seized and the *hamster* summoned to appear in court. Thus, we prudently chose rainy or at least cloudy days for our trips to Lövenich. This allowed us to wear trench coats without arousing undue suspicion. Beneath the ample girth of this garment dangled a pound of ham, half a dozen carefully wrapped eggs, and a bag of potatoes, beans, and flour, all hanging from strings slung across our shoulders or tied to a belt. When we got off the train, we tried to walk with a springy gait that belied both the weight of the unlawful haul hidden under our raincoats and the anxiety of our hearts. Once safely home, there was joy and jubilation. We could look forward to seven fat days after seven times seven lean days.

But hamstering was child's play compared to the Wild West atmosphere along the frontier near the city. Thousands of people tried to cross into Belgium through the prohibited area or no-man's land, to bring back coffee, unobtainable in Germany, dirt cheap in Belgium. Some merely wanted a pound or two for the pleasure of indulging in a rare taste treat or, more likely, for trade against real necessities. But there were those who smuggled on a large scale, for profit. They dealt in hundreds, yes thousands of pounds, and made their daring trips in fake Red Cross vans, hearses with coffee-filled coffins, and even in armored cars. Bitches in heat were used to distract the dogs of the Frontier Control Service. The so-called crow's-feet—curved hooks, one of whose spiked ends always pointed up—tore holes in the tires of pursuing customs vehicles. Several times, there were deadly shootouts on this coffee front.

We, of course, had strict orders from our parents to stay away from the border. Hermann broke this taboo once. He made his way to Astenet where Mother had spent some weeks recuperating from a serious illness in the quiet of a convent surrounded by a beautiful garden. When he returned with butter, coffee, and greetings from the nuns, he reaped, instead of the expected thanks, a fearful thrashing. He did not do it again.

At last, after Easter 1946, I was able to go back to gymnasium. No boy had ever waited with greater impatience for the end of vacation than I, but then *my* vacation had been permanent. Or so it seemed, since I had not attended school in a year and a half. And my education prior to that had been erratic, to say the least.

A pleasant surprise was in store for me at registration time. I was conditionally admitted to the *Untersekunda*, the fourth grade of gymnasium, though I had hardly set foot in the third except for digging some useless ditches near Kempen. Uncle Anton's pedagogic efforts, my knowledge of English honed in conversations with Joseph and the first group of officers quartered in our house, Herr Jussen's learned disquisitions on the vital role of music in society (and thus, incidentally, of extra food rations for opera singers), and my voracious independent reading had borne fruit: The war did not cost me a whole year in school. I was given a chance to prove myself in the *Untersekunda*.

Classes ran in three shifts: morning, midday, and late afternoon because one usable school building had to serve three separate gymnasiums. If we wanted to be warm in winter, everyone brought a briquette or a log to fuel the classroom stove. Paper and pencils were scarce, books few, laboratory supplies nonexisting, and stomachs perpetually rumbling on 1,050 calories per day, but we were not about to let such obstacles stand in our way. After the nightmare of senseless slaughter and destruction, we longed to move forward. We had conjured up, from our midst, the macabre piper of hell, danced the dance of death to his strident tune, and wound up paying with at least part of our souls. Now we were all eager to begin anew, to build, to heal, and to create. And so, with little more than the four bare walls of the classroom, teachers and students together wove a magic atmosphere of intellectual excitement and ferment that none of us will ever forget.

Not much time was spent discussing the Third Reich. We had all lived through it, barely, first attracted and finally repelled by its diabolical glitter. Blinded by Lucifer, we had fallen into a fiery abyss from where we had only just returned, burnt but purified in a cathartic conflagration. Instinctively we knew that the past had been left behind, reduced to ashes. Our hearts and minds were open to the future now, waiting to discover a world of meaning beyond the sham of Nazism.

CHAPTER 29

One thing remained to be done before Hitler's ghost was forever put to rest in our family: Father still had to be *denazified*. By order of the Allied Control Council, all adult Germans were to be divided into five groups, ranging from category I, *Major Offenders*, to category V, *Persons Exonerated*. In between fell the intermediate rankings of *Offenders, Lesser Offenders*, and *Fellow Travelers*, and lest this classification should prove too broad to measure all conceivable gradations in individual guilt, these headings were further subdivided into some two-dozen subcategories. *Cuique suum*. The new democratic order was to be built on numerous classes of citizenship corresponding to each man's exact standing on the denazification ladder.

Questionnaires went out to the far corners of the land. The answers, together with other incriminating evidence, were to serve as the basis for judging everybody's degree of criminal, political, or moral guilt for the crimes of the Third Reich.

The Inquisition soon found itself buried under millions of cases, most of them inconsequential. With no time for public hearings and little concern for any of the finer points of the rules of evidence, the denazification tribunals tried to dispense a sort of rough and ready justice, assigning each citizen to one of the categories according to the deeds he had done or the beliefs he had harbored or the organizations he had belonged to during the Hitler years.

One Sunday morning, I attended mass in a church near the city. I had left home early on a hamstering expedition, my mind being preoccupied with mundane visions of flour and potatoes. Thus, I was totally unprepared for the miracle of reincarnation I was about to witness. The moment I caught sight of the sacristan making his way through the crowded house of God, I sensed with an eerie but absolute certainty that I had met this man before, under different circumstances, in a different life. I wracked my brains to determine when and where our paths had crossed. In vain, I could not remember.

Suddenly the blinders fell from my eyes. I was dumbfounded. This man, in sackcloth and ashes, with the sunken, penitent eyes, with the prayerful lips mumbling pious responses, with the shuffling gait befitting his present occupation, was none other than the speaker who had addressed our *Jungvolk* meeting one evening before Christmas not long ago. That day he had worn a brown shirt with armband and swastika. His mien had been haughty, his stride proud and strutting in high boots. His ringing voice had proclaimed unwavering loyalty to the Führer. The glad tidings of peace and joy at Christmas, he told us, were meant only for people of good will, not for vermin like Jews, subhumans, cowards, or traitors. "Today, there is a wider meaning to Christmas. It symbolizes the redemption of the world through Adolf Hitler, who was sent to us by God. We have come together to celebrate the winter solstice, when the long night threatens to overwhelm the short day, but as surely as light will triumph over darkness and as the sun will bring us again a glorious, radiant day, so we will destroy the hordes of our enemies. For we love our Führer and are willing to sacrifice ourselves just as Jesus had to die to fulfill his mission. Peace and joy to all men of good will." And he concluded by making us sing a new Christmas song, which he called especially appropriate *today as we pass through a solstitial turning point in our nation's fate.*

> Deutschland, sieh uns, wir weihen
> dir den Tod als kleinste Tat;
> grüsst er einst unsre Reihen,
> werden wir die grosse Saat.

> Germany, we consecrate, faithful and solemn,
> our death to you, as our smallest deed;

watch us; if death greets our column,
we will turn into a mighty seed.

Though at that time I had still been vulnerable to some of the seductive nonsense of Nazism, I had instinctively shrunk back from this reinterpretation of Christmas, which filled me with deep anxiety. I harbored no secret death wish and neither did our speaker, for here he was, well and alive, having found refuge in the all-encompassing bosom of the church. I could not take my eyes off the sacristan. What a transformation between that winter solstice and this Sunday morning.

Aachen lay in the British zone of occupation where many of the formerly most rabid Nazis could, like the sacristan, avoid an unfavorable classification in a denazification proceeding by lying low until the storm had blown over. Father, however, in order to regain his full civil rights, petitioned a tribunal to take up his case.

He was placed in category IV, *Fellow Traveler*, but assigned to a low subcategory. As a result, he had to pay a fine and was forbidden to reopen his business.

I was outraged. Surely, one of Father's competitors, tempted by a lust for mammon, had borne false witness against him. I knew quite a few loudmouthed Nazis who had received better classifications than he, with no restrictions on their freedom. In fact, the German tribunals in the British zone put almost everybody into category V, *Exonerated Persons*, and did not even have the right to put anyone into categories I or II because the military authorities were supposed to deal with these criminals. But the British had failed to pick up many *Major Offenders*, who had successfully covered their tracks, so that the German denazification tribunals were finally forced to classify these people as *Lesser Offenders*, in category III. Why had they given Father a number IV, just one notch above the worst culprits? Why was he not placed in category V where he belonged? I had never seen him do anything wrong and had never heard him defend Hitler's sinister policies. Because of him, I had not been *educated* in an *Adolf Hitler Schule* and kept at least part of my head out of the quagmire of Nazi ideology. "This kind of justice is no better than that of the Third Reich!" I shouted.

Father would have none of that. Though he was bitter, too, he kept a sense of proportion. He believed in the necessity of denazification to punish the guilty and to purge public life of those who had made the major decisions and had participated directly in criminal actions, but the net had been cast too widely so that many little fish were caught whose fault was more a question of moral failure and political error than of criminal guilt. He did not think any of his rivals had denounced him. It was more likely that the denazifiers had simply looked at the year of his entry into the *NSDAP* and concluded he was a pretty bad case because he had joined so early. Of course, he could not be sure since no reasons were given by the tribunal for its decision.

Father and I talked late that night about his career in the Party. He had joined in 1932 when it enjoyed a bogus air of respectability. Big industry, finance, and the managerial classes were flocking to its support, and the traditional parties of the *Weimar Republic* seemed incapable of governing effectively. "I am certainly not proud of what I did," he explained. "It was an entirely negative act, a vote *against* the chaos of the times rather than *for* anything in particular. It was based on the vague hope that *any* change had to be an improvement. I soon learned otherwise, but it was too late. There was close surveillance of our political loyalty down to each cell and block. I would have been a marked man had I taken the drastic step of advertising my misgivings by quitting the Party. So I chose the easy way and stayed. I paid my dues and visited the wounded. That was about it, but even so, I must bear part of our collective responsibility for allowing Hitler to come to power and rule with our consent. My first and perhaps biggest mistake was to enter a party about which I knew very little."

Father paused for a moment and then finished with this advice, "Never, never join a group without thoroughly investigating its values, its goals, and above all, the character of its leaders. If I had read *Mein Kampf* before 1932, I would never have been a Nazi."

I was still angry with the denazification tribunal. It seemed stupid to assign a greater degree of responsibility to those who had fallen for Hitler in 1932 than in, say, 1940, for with each passing year the criminal policies of the regime had become more evident. In a way, I thought, the *later* one had joined, the guiltier he was.

Father disdained getting himself a *whitewash slip*, *Persilschein* in German, named after the well-known laundry detergent. This was a statement from a prominent non-Nazi, often a priest, testifying to a person's upright character and the righteous convictions he had exhibited, during the Third Reich, in spite of formal membership in the Party. Such an exculpation certificate would normally help a petitioner to be moved into a better category. It would have been easy for Father to obtain a *Persilschein* since he had remained an active, practicing Catholic throughout the Hitler years, but he stubbornly insisted on having his case reviewed on the basis of the facts before the tribunal.

The wheels of justice grind slowly. Month after month went by while we waited for a decision on his appeal. At last, the day of judgment was upon us. Father was reclassified. The denazifiers had concluded that the world was safe for democracy even with a man of his character running a retail store in the city of Aachen.

CHAPTER 30

Despite the fascination school held for me, it did not occupy all my time. Hermann and I spent many hours digging through the rubble in the Grosskölnstrasse, picking out unbroken bricks, knocking off the mortar, and stacking them in neat piles. Not a single one was ever used in the reconstruction of our own house. Still, our efforts did contribute toward that distant goal, although in a roundabout way. We traded the cleaned but still antique-looking bricks, at the rate of one of ours for two brand-new ones, to a seventeenth-century pub. It, too, had been destroyed during the war, and to rebuild it in style, old bricks were, of course, needed. Later, whenever I visited the *Postwagen* to sip a beer in its faithfully restored historical setting, I had the smug feeling of sitting between my own four walls.

Another project of mine was to put to use the gardening skills I had acquired in Kempen under Uncle Anton's tutelage. The only available space was a tiny, enclosed yard behind the house in the Saarstrasse whose main purpose was to hold numerous garbage cans. A thin strip of arid soil along the walls supported a few sickly weeds. This unpromising patch of earth, almost totally shielded from the sun, would have to serve as my garden.

But first, I had to prepare the site. On the Salvatorberg, I dug up a wheelbarrow full of soil, which I enriched with manure easily collected by trailing the many horse-drawn carriages that had replaced automobile traffic in the city.

It would be an exaggeration to say my garden produced a prolific crop, but I did manage to nurse along half a dozen tomatoes, enough beans for several meals, and some heads of lettuce. These made me especially proud, for Mother was more addicted to greens than any rabbit I had ever seen.

In December 1947, Mother had miraculously assembled all the ingredients for a special Christmas cake. She baked an enormous *Stollen* filled with raisins, almonds, and fruit but mercifully devoid of elderberries. When it was done, she embellished its steaming, light-brown crust with a dusting of powdered sugar and then hid the finished masterpiece somewhere in the apartment.

Its whereabouts could not long remain secret. As soon as I was alone, my nose led me to the living room where, from one of the locked compartments of the buffet, emanated the unmistakable aroma of the *Stollen*. But where was the key? It would be such a pleasure just to look at the cake, to admire its perfection, to feast on its sweet smell from close by.

A determined search produced the key in the drawer of Mother's bedside table. I reverently approached the shrine holding the precious object and unlocked the door. A shocking sight awaited me: The lovely long loaf had been nibbled and gnawed at both ends, its immaculate beauty violated by ravenous teeth. No doubt Marita and Hermann had already preceded me. Thus, I reasoned, there was no need for any further self-restraint, and I boldly broke off two hefty chunks. Delicious!

A week passed before I had a chance to check again on the condition of the *Stollen*. This time, I was not surprised to find it had suffered another substantial shrinkage. Once again, I helped myself to a generous pre-Christmas tasting.

Next evening, Mother put the sadly mutilated cake on the dinner table. "I want to know who has done this," she said. Nobody was willing to take the blame, but Marita suggested a mouse had been at work. Her need to offer such an implausible explanation confirmed my suspicion that she was the chief culprit in the case of the dwindling *Stollen*. After all, she had the sweetest tooth and the best opportunity to taste of the forbidden cake since the living room doubled as her bedroom. What could be harder than to sleep in such tempting proximity to the object of her desire without succumbing?

Mother, though annoyed, joined in the general laughter that greeted Marita's answer. She did not insist on finding out the truth. "Let's forget what has happened. From now on, the *Stollen* will be in the kitchen cabinet, unlocked. It's up to you to decide whether you want to enjoy and share it together with all of us on Christmas day or gulp it down whenever you are alone. Please, don't disappoint me."

The cake was not touched again until December 25. We three children and the unjustly incriminated mice respected Mother's plea.

I think this was the last incident of food filching in our family, for in June of 1948, the *German miracle* began. In truth, there was something utterly miraculous in the suddenness with which all kinds of things, hitherto unobtainable, reappeared on the market for sale.

Three friends and I had long been planning a trip up the Rhine, across the Black Forest and back through the Neckar Valley. With ingenuity and hard work, we had patched together four bicycles from old parts found here and there. Then, just before our departure, the currency reform wiped out all existing money, replacing the plentiful but worthless *Reichsmark* with scarce *Deutsche Mark*. Initially every household received DM 60 for the head and DM 40 for each member of a family. We spent a night persuading our parents to let us have thirty marks and next morning set forth on our journey. By late afternoon, we were sitting on the terrace of a restaurant overlooking the Rhine. Never shall I forget my amazement when, for fifty pfennige apiece, we were served a bottle of excellent wine and treated with flattering courtesy and respect. Nor will I ever forget the bustling marketplace of a small town where sellers eagerly tried to push their fruit, vegetables, cheese, and even chickens on an excited crowd of cautious customers. For just pennies, I bought more tomatoes than my miserable garden would ever produce. Such was the wondrous power of the new money. When I returned home after three weeks, I still had over five marks left in my pocket.

The currency reform unleashed the economy. Suddenly the pace of reconstruction quickened. The wheels of industry spun twice as fast. Controls withered away. The *Wirtschaftswunder* (economic miracle) put to work the ranks of the unemployed swollen by the influx of refugees who had been expelled from their homelands in the east. In short order, production surpassed all previous records, overcoming both the devastation of war and the postwar dismantling of many factories.

This was what most people mean when they speak of the *German miracle*. But to me, it had come to mean something entirely different. Just the day before yesterday, so it seemed to me, I had joined the *Jungvolk* and longed for promotion to *Hordenführer*, for enrollment in the *Adolf Hitler Schule*, for service as a *Luftwaffenhelfer*, and in one dark moment, even for total war. Only yesterday I had walked, dazed, through the wasteland of my city, unable to imagine that there would ever again be a world without ruins. Yet all around me, a new world was springing up, and the people creating it were the same men and women who had so docilely followed the Führer, some knowingly, others blindly. Some had been idealistic, some power hungry; some earnest, others reckless; some innocent, many guilty. But today, all were working together to forge a decent, caring, free society.

I almost admired my fellow countrymen for their courage, patience, strength, and resilience. Somehow I could not believe that they were innately worse than other people. We had the same potential for good and for evil. For twelve long years, evil had run wild, unchecked, ensnaring us all in the tendrils of its rank, luxuriant growth, but it had not choked off the other half. That was the *real* miracle for me.

Once again, I thought of the words of Anne Frank, "In spite of everything, I still believe in the good of man."

Epilogue

Why did Nazism arise in Germany? It would be comforting to believe it could not have happened anywhere else because there was something unique in the course of German history or in the German national character which allowed this virulent ideology to thrive in only that one nation. We know better today. The seeds of kindred ugly movements can be seen sprouting in many places. The rest of the world is by no means immune from the disease—witness the insulting inflammatory language used by right-wing demagogues and even by some government leaders against refugees, migrants, and any newcomers who are *different*.

Sadly, history is full of examples of man's inhumanity to man and not just of isolated crimes of mob violence but of monstrous, systematic atrocities of group against group. We need only think of the tens of millions of Africans who were hunted, slaughtered, or captured to be sold into slavery. Or of the Turkish massacre of the Armenians, or the unspeakable terror imposed by Stalin on the Soviet Union, or of Pol Pot and the Khmer Rouge turning their country into a killing field where perhaps a quarter of the Cambodian population perished.

The list could go on and on. These few illustrations, however, are more than enough to make it sickeningly clear how common mass murder and the trampling of the dignity of man have been in the annals of history.

Yet we must firmly resist the temptation of trying to extenuate the enormity of human atrocities by comparing them to what others have done. Besides, what happened in Germany during the Hitler years was different not only in the scale but also in the very nature of the crimes committed. First, all Jews were slandered, humiliated, and deprived of their rights, and then they were herded into holding pens called concentration camps. And, finally, in the pursuit of the *Endlösung* (final solution), they were shipped off to death factories where the extermination of millions of people could be carried out on an industrial scale. In this way, the mechanization of death rose to a pinnacle of infamy hitherto unknown.

In spite of all this, I reject the idea that we are inherently evil. Certainly, we carry within ourselves the potential for evil, but we are also endowed with a boundless capacity for good. How then are we to explain the fact that the powers of darkness so often eclipse the light of the world?

At least part of the answer lies in the political institutions and traditions of different countries. Wherever democracy thrives, hatred and violence cannot rule unchallenged. I am not so naïve as to believe that democratic nations have not been, and will not be again, guilty of heinous crimes against humanity, but when people are free, they will sooner or later recognize evil for what it is. Many will take a stand against it so that a measure of reason and decency may prevail in the end. Sometimes the wait may be excruciatingly long, yet even in the blackest night, the torch of hope will not be fully extinguished. Such countries are never without a conscience. Eventually, their citizens will be roused into action, supporting what is right, opposing what is blatantly wrong.

Edmund Burke has said, "The only thing necessary for the triumph of evil is for good men to do nothing." It is perhaps the greatest virtue of democracy that it is a system which makes it relatively safe for us to fight against evil. One does not have to be a hero to do so in a free country. To be sure, dissent has its costs, but these do not exceed the price that honorable men of strength and character are prepared to pay. They may face ridicule, economic hardship, harassment, and even persecution. They do not, however, expect to be tortured, shut up in a concentration camp or gulag, or put to a cruel death.

In all nations, at all times, there are many people of good will. Democracy provides an institutional framework within which their voices can be heard. In a dictatorship, by contrast, it is often not enough to be good. You must be a hero as well, ready to risk everything to prevent the triumph of evil. And heroes are scarce everywhere. They are called upon to show extraordinary courage while most of us, alas, are made of ordinary clay.

Thus, the wonder is not how few heroes there are in totalitarian states but how many. They are lonely voices crying in the wilderness, doomed to perish for upholding the simple standards of decency and humanity. These men and women may not succeed in changing their country's disastrous course as, for example, Stalin and Hitler's opponents failed in their efforts to check the reign of terror. Yet their sacrifices are never in vain. Through them, what is worthy and noble in a nation's tradition is kept alive.

It was a tragedy for the world that German citizens before 1933 showed so little devotion to the principles of democracy that they allowed the fragile Weimar Republic to slide, almost without a struggle, into an all-powerful party dictatorship. Once this change was completed, organized opposition would become almost impossible. Only heroic individuals with a deep moral commitment like Pastor Dietrich Bonhoeffer or small groups like the *Weisse Rose* (White Rose) centered around the brother and sister Hans and Sophie Scholl, dared to oppose, peacefully, the evils of the regime, and they were ruthlessly sentenced to death by Nazi-controlled courts. Alas, the number of heroes like these proved woefully unequal to the immensity of the task, but even during those thirteen years, there were millions of good people in Germany. In a society afraid and intolerant of free inquiry, most were ensnared and deluded. Many did not know the full extent of their country's crimes, and if they knew, they did not know what to do about it without exposing themselves and their families to incalculable risks. And so they withdrew into a private world of goodness, leaving evil free to run rampant in the public domain. For this, they are guilty, my parents as well as most Germans of their generation.

No doubt, some wrongs would have been committed even in a non-Nazi Germany, for prejudice, bigotry, and chauvinism were rife at that time. But surely, the worst outrages could not have occurred if the self-corrective forces of democracy had been at work. Can anyone conceive of a free people saying yes to the mass murder of their Jewish fellow men?

Like most Germans alive today, I am too young to feel any personal guilt for the crimes of the Hitler years. Our responsibility is not so much for what happened but for how we are going to deal with it. We must accept the consequences of our nation's past. Neither we nor the generations to come should ever let this darkest period in our history be forgotten. It is a burden we must bear, willingly. It is a stain that will forever tarnish the name of Germany. Above all, we must learn from it, and one important lesson is that democracy, for all its imperfections, offers the best and perhaps the only hope that good men will not allow evil to triumph absolutely. Thus, it becomes a moral imperative for men and women everywhere to preserve and strengthen democratic institutions.

What would I—or you—have done if fate had willed us to live as adult citizens in the Third Reich? I can only hope I would have found within myself the courage to resist with fearless determination, but I humbly recognize the likelihood that I might simply have been a *good* German in private, doing little or nothing to stop the Führer.

And so I am sad, infinitely sad, about what happened in Germany, but I cannot condemn the entire previous generation. I have not earned the right to do so. My willingness to risk all has not yet been put to the test since I have never been forced to choose between doing what is right and losing my life.

About the Author

Herbert A. Goertz was born in Aachen, Germany, in 1932. He studied at Cologne University and, as a Fulbright Exchange Student, at Bowling Green State University and Yale University where he taught for two years. He then moved to New England and continued teaching for many years at Dartmouth College, Royalton Law Study Center, and Royalton College as well as at the Mountain School in Vershire, Vermont. He and his wife live in Central Vermont on a hill farm with a view of the Green Mountains.

CPSIA information can be obtained
at www.ICGtesting.com
Printed in the USA
LVHW101923040423
743437LV00002B/427